MW01600505

Far Past the Frontier

Far Past the Frontier

James A. Braden

FAR PAST THE FRONTIER

Published in the United States by IndyPublish.com
Boston, Massachusetts

ISBN 1-4378-9082-2 (paperback)

CONTENTS

CHAPTER I.

The Flight of Big Pete Ellis.

"Look out thar!"

A young, red-bearded man of herculean frame fiercely jerked the words between his teeth as he leaped between two boys who were about to enter the country store, from the door of which he sprang.

Diving aside, but quickly turning, the lads saw the cause of their sudden movement bound into a wagon standing near, and with a furious cry to the horses, whip them to such instant, rapid speed that the strap with which the animals were tied, snapped like a bit of string. With a clatter and rumbling roar the team and wagon dashed around a corner, the clumsy vehicle all but upsetting, as the wheels on one side flew clear of the ground.

Running forward, the boys were in time to see, fast disappearing down the road toward where the September sun was setting, the reckless driver bending over, lashing the horses to a frantic gallop. The wagon swayed and jolted over the ruts and holes, threatening momentarily to throw the fellow headlong. An empty barrel in the box bounced up and down and from side to side like a thing alive.

"Something has happened! Big Pete isn't doing that for fun!" the larger of the boys exclaimed.

"Run for Dr. Cartwright, quick! Big Pete has killed Jim Huson, I'm afraid!"

The speaker was Marvel Rice, proprietor of the store in which Huson was a clerk. "Tell him to hurry—hurry!" the merchant cried again, as without a second's hesitation the two boys sped away along the tan-bark path.

"Are you coming, Ree?" asked the more slender lad, glancing over his shoulder with a droll smile. He was a wiry chap of sixteen and ran like a grey hound, easily taking the lead.

His companion made no reply, but his spirit fired by the sarcastic question, he forged ahead, and the other found it necessary to waste no more breath in humor.

An admirer of youthful strength and development would have clapped his hands with delight to have seen the boys' close race. Return Kingdom, whom the slender lad had called "Ree," was a tall, strongly built, muscular fellow of seventeen. His fine black hair waved under the brim of a dilapidated beaver as he ran. His brown eyes were serious and keen and his mouth and chin emphasized the determination expressed in them. Though his clothes were of rough home-spun stuff, and his feet were encased in coarse boots, an observing person would have seen that he was possessed of the decision and strength in both mind and body which go to make leaders among men.

The smaller boy was John Jerome—quick, vigorous, brown-haired, blue-eyed, freckled, and his attire was like that of his companion whose follower he was in everything save foot-racing. In that he would give way to no one, not excluding the trained Indian runners who sometimes came to the neighboring village.

"Easy, easy!" Dr. Cartwright sang out, the boys nearly colliding with him as he was driving from his dooryard. "Somebody dying?" he asked as the runners halted.

"Jim Huson's been hurt; they want you at the store, quick," Ree Kingdom breathlessly explained.

"Badly?" asked the doctor with provoking deliberation, drawing on his gloves.

"Pretty nigh killed, I guess; Big Pete Ellis did it," put in John Jerome, amazed that the physician did not at once drive off at lightning speed.

"And they want me to finish the job do they?" smiled Dr. Cartwright, who was never known to become excited. "Well, I'll see what I can do. Daisy, get up."

The latter words were for the faithful mare that had drawn the doctor's chaise, or two-wheeled carriage, summer and winter for so many years that she was as well known as the physician himself. The horse set off at a leisurely jog, but the master's second "Get up Daisy," though drawled out as if haste were the last thing to be thought of, quickened the animal's speed to a lively trot.

The boys started back at a walk, speculating on what could have provoked Big Pete's assault and how serious Jim Huson's injury might be.

"It upsets all our plans," said John; "for Jim was just the fellow to tell us the price of everything and just what western emigrants should take along. We can't talk to Mr. Rice about our going, as we could talk to Jim."

"Mr. Rice is so excitable he may have thought Huson worse hurt than he is," Ree answered. "Anyway, we are not to start for three weeks, and Jim may be up and around long before we go. So don't be blue. There is more than one way to skin a cat. If we can't have Jim's advice we can talk with some one else, or use our own judgment as to what we must buy. In the end we will have to depend entirely on ourselves as to what we should or should not do, anyway; but come what may, three weeks from this very Monday, we shall go, if we live and have our health."

"Bully for you, Ree! In three weeks our faces will be turned toward the setting sun!"

"Our backs will be toward the rising sun in three weeks, less one day," Ree answered. "But scamper along; let's get back to the store and find out first how Jim was hurt and how badly. It will be a sorry job for Pete Ellis, if they catch him."

The assault on the clerk at the Corners' store had aroused the neighborhood. Coming at the hour of sundown when the day's work was nearly over, it found people with leisure to hurry to the scene to learn all about the affair. A dozen men and boys and a few women and children were gathered near when Return Kingdom and John Jerome arrived. The boys found that their injured friend had been carried to the inn across the street, where Dr. Cartwright was attending him, and all were anxiously waiting that good man's opinion.

The story of the assault as it was told, over and over again, as the crowd about the store increased, was that Big Pete had attempted to pass counterfeit money on Jim Huson. The latter refused it, accusing Ellis of having brought spurious coin to him at other times as well, and threatening to cause his arrest. Without warning Big Pete seized a heavy butter firkin and threw it squarely at the clerk's head.

Huson dropped unconscious to the floor, and Mr. Rice, who ran to his aid, received a similar blow. Ellis lost no time in dashing through the open door, then adding to his other crimes the theft of horses and wagon to assist in his escape.

"Well, there is no great loss without some small gain," said one man. "We are quit of Big Pete, that's certain, and it is a good riddance of bad rubbish. He was the worst man in this bailiwick, and I am thinking that more than one job of pilfering might safely be laid at his door."

It was, indeed, true. Big Pete was not looked upon as a desirable citizen. So bad had his name become that he could scarcely find employment where he was known. The honest people of old Connecticut had little liking for dishonesty, notwithstanding the stories of the money-making ingenuity of that state's inhabitants.

Leaning against a post, apart from the other men, Ree Kingdom presently noticed an aged farmer, alternately wringing his hands and burying his face in them. He was the owner of the team which had been stolen, and, heedless of all else idly lamented his loss, complaining that no one went in pursuit of the thief to secure his horses, but wholly forgetful of the best of scriptural proverbs that God helps those who help themselves. The boy was about to speak to him, when two men dashed up on horseback.

"There's the constable," John Jerome exclaimed—"The constable and his brother, and they are going after Big Pete."

Before Ree could answer, the officer called for volunteers to assist in his undertaking, for Ellis was known to be a dangerous man.

"Here, some of you young bucks that can ride bare-back, strip the harness off my team an' help ketch that murderous heathen! Only wish't I wasn't all crippled up with rheumatics, I'd show him!"

The speaker was Captain William Bowen, who had fought in the Revolutionary War, ending seven years earlier, (1783) and was proud of it; and who, though really sadly crippled by rheumatism, was still a sure shot and not the man to be trifled with by law-breakers. He would permit no one to call him anything but "Captain." His old rifle was always within reach and two big pistols were ever his companions.

For a minute no one made a move to accept the captain's offer, and then with: "Come on, John," Ree Kingdom waited no longer. In a twinkling the boys unharnessed the horses, leaving only the bridles on them, and were mounted. Tom Huson, the blacksmith and Peter Piper, a half-breed Indian, a sort of roustabout in the neighborhood, had also hurriedly prepared to join in the chase.

"Take my twins, lads, they bite as hard as they bark," called Captain Bowen, passing his brace of pistols up to Ree and John, and in another moment the party was galloping in pursuit of the big fellow whose crime might yet be murder, Dr. Cartwright having reported that only time could tell.

"Who-ho-ho-ho-ho!" John Jerome could not resist the temptation to give an Indian war-whoop. There is an exhilaration in a rapid ride by moonlight at any time, and with the clatter of the hoofs of a half dozen horses upon the beaten road, the forms of other riders, shadowy and ghost-like on either side to lend a feeling of companionship, and a knowledge of danger's presence to make every sense the more alert, there is no finer excitement. Little wonder is it that John could not repress a yell, and though of a much quieter disposition, Ree felt like shouting, also.

"Who-ho-ho-ho!" John yelled again, a half hour later, and the women and children ran to the door of a house they were passing to see who it might be that was dashing by at such breakneck speed. The air came soft and cool to the riders half hidden in the shadows of the trees which bordered the road, though the moon was shining gloriously.

"We will send you on ahead to tell Pete we are coming, if you are so fond of making it known, youngster," exclaimed the constable as John gave still another whoop.

"He'd have a cat fit if he knew you were after him, I'll wager," the boy answered, nettled by the man's sarcasm. "Suppose I do ride on and let him know."

John leaned back and slapped his horse's flank. The animal, scarcely more than a colt, sprang forward at great speed. At the same time the young rider raised up on his knees, then on his feet and keeping his balance with seeming ease, standing nearly erect, the horse running its fastest, he held the reins in one hand, waved his hat in the other, and again yelled like an Indian.

"That young dare-devil will kill himself one of these days," said the blacksmith. "That colt of Captain Bowen's is likely to take it into her head to bring up short at any minute. Better call him back, Kingdom."

Ree had no fear that his friend could not take care of himself, but in answer to the suggestion, he gave a shrill, peculiar whistle which made the woodland ring. Like a shot John dropped to a sitting posture as he heard the call, and in another minute Ree had ridden up beside him. Before either could speak, a black object loomed up in the narrow road and they had barely time to rein their horses in before they were upon it, the animals leaping sidewise to avoid a collision.

"Big Pete's wagon, sure as shooting! It's broken down!" ejaculated Ree.

"Scotland! Where would I have landed if I had been standing up and this colt had run into it?" John exclaimed. As he spoke the others of their party came up.

"Here's the wagon, but Pete and the horses are gone," called Ree. "He can't be far ahead."

"There's no telling. Hurry on," answered the constable who had hastily sprung off his horse to examine the wreck. "Here are the harnesses, but Pete is trying to get away with both horses. Keep your wits about you, boys, there is likely to be some shooting!"

Ree had been the first to start forward, and was one hundred yards in advance of the others when his quick eye detected the dim outlines of a man on horseback in the shadow of a low branching oak just before him at the roadside. He recognized the huge figure of Big Pete and without a word guided his horse straight toward the fellow. The criminal saw him and with a yell started off.

Ree's horse with a splendid bound cleared the ditch beside the highway, and in another moment the boy had seized the bridle of the horse Big Pete was leading, just as the fellow was getting the animal he bestrode under rapid way for a race for his liberty. It was clear that he had been delayed by the breaking down of the wagon, and had hidden at the roadside hoping his pursuers would pass him by. With a determined grip Ree clung to the bridle of the lead horse, though he was nearly jerked to the ground. With his other hand he sought to check his own animal, but the skittish young thing had taken fright and was now running ahead of the flying criminal's horses.

A great out-cry came from the constable and his party as they saw what had happened and dug spurs into their mounts. Down the road the pursued and pursuers raced, Ree Kingdom wholly unable to retard Big Pete's progress but still clinging to the bridle of the horse between them, the constable and his men trying their best to overtake the fugitive, but unable to gain on him.

"Shoot! why don't you shoot?" yelled Ree to his friends at last, and a pair of pistols cracked simultaneously, a third and fourth rapidly following.

Ree heard the bullets whistle near his head and realized that he was in almost as much danger of being hit, as Big Pete. But again he cried:

"Shoot!"

The pursuers were slowly but surely falling behind in the race. The burly Ellis, glancing back, was quick to see that fortune favored him. He leaned far over from his horse and before Ree Kingdom could detect his purpose in the dusky light, seized the boy by the neck. With a giant's strength he pulled the lad partially from his seat, endeavoring to hurl him to the ground. Failing, he relinquished his hold on the reins, and using both hands, succeeded in drawing Kingdom over the unridden horse between them to the shoulders of his own horse. And then with herculean efforts he tried to throw the boy to the earth.

But Ree held to his own horse's reins with bull dog ferocity, and with all his strength resisted the other's effort. As he was jerked from his seat, however, the strain on the reins caused his horse to sharply swerve inward, crowding against the other animals, and in a twinkling the three of them, already frantic with the fury of their wild race, left the course and sped across a woodland at the unfenced roadside.

Gasping an oath, the enraged giant tried again to push Ree to the ground, and this time he succeeded; but he himself went off head-foremost with the boy, who held to his arm with a grip of steel, dragging him suddenly down. Freed of their burden, the horses ran on, Big Pete cursing frightfully as he sprang to his feet to find them far beyond his reach.

Lying still, bruised but not seriously hurt by his fall, Ree Kingdom was thinking fast. He felt for his pistol inspired by the thought that he would capture the criminal yet, and wishing he had used it earlier. But the weapon was gone—lost in the wild ride, no doubt. The next instant Ellis swiftly turned and seized him by the throat; and he knew that his life was in the giant's hands.

CHAPTER II.

A Bound Boy's Story.

With the horses gone beyond recapture, Big Pete must needs depend on his own legs if he meant to escape. The constable's party could not be far behind, and with the boy, whose throat he clutched, to point the way in which he had gone, when the officer came up, his chance of getting away was much less than it would be should that boy be powerless to give any information.

Ree Kingdom thought of this and lay perfectly still, feigning insensibility but keenly wondering what disposition would be made of him, and resolved to fight to the last breath if his pretense of unconsciousness were discovered. Then the giant's grip about his throat grew tighter, and he felt that a terrible struggle and perhaps death were just at hand. Between his almost closed eyelids he saw the man's big frame bending silently over him and thus moments which seemed like hours passed.

The slow-thinking fugitive could not at once decide what he should do. He was hoping Ree would spring to his feet and run. Then, pretending to try to catch him, he would escape among the darker shadows before the boy could see in which direction he had gone. He was not deceived by the pretense of unconsciousness, as Ree thought, and really hoped to be saved the necessity of killing the lad or of knocking him senseless, to a certainty, lest such a blow might produce death. He shuddered as he remembered that his hands were probably already stained with blood.

If Ellis had but known it, flight was far from Kingdom's thoughts. He was steadfast in his every purpose, to a fault, and having set out to capture Big Pete, the idea of running away just as he was face to face with the giant fellow, did not so much as occur to him, though he well knew his peril.

"Scoot!" With sudden fury Ellis dragged Ree to his feet and violently pushed him as he spoke, expecting to see the boy dash away.

Ree could not prevent a grim smile from crossing his lips as he turned quickly toward the giant again, realizing that the fellow had intended to frighten him. Each moment, however, he looked for a deadly conflict to begin, and as he stood in quiet defiance, trying to determine what the fugitive's next move would be, and momentarily expecting a struggle, there was in the background of his thoughts a vision of an unmarked, flower-strewn grave in a quiet church-yard. Strongly intertwined with it was memory of his past life. But hark!

"Clockety-clack-clockety-clack!" It was the sound of horses' hoofs close by. The constable had discovered them at last. Big Pete heard the hoof-beats and knew he had paused too long.

"Death to ye!" he cried with an oath, and lodged a hammer-like blow on Kingdom's head, sending the lad staggering, while he swiftly took to his heels.

Dazed, but still conscious, Ree sprang after him, shouting "Come on!" to the party of horsemen now but a few rods distant, "Ellis has just this minute run into the woods!"

For an hour the men searched for the fugitive, but in vain. He had disappeared completely and in the deep darkness pervading the thickly-grown brush and trees of the forest he eluded his pursuers with ease.

In disappointment the chase was abandoned and attention given to capturing the escaped horses. This was at last accomplished, and as the early moon was waning, the constable and his volunteers turned homeward. One source of satisfaction was theirs—they had, at least, recovered the stolen team and wagon, though the latter would need many repairs before again being fit for service.

Ree briefly told of his adventure as the party rode along. John Jerome could not withhold his words of regret that his horse had been too slow for the race, nor could he quite understand how the stolen team had been able to outstrip the others.

"I'll tell you how that was," said the constable's brother. "The nags Big Pete had was really runnin' away. I guess you know how much faster a dog will run when he has a rattle tied to his tail, than when he's jest runnin' for the fun on it! Wall, this here's a parallel case."

Although it was nearly midnight, a small crowd of curious ones was found still lingering about Mr. Rice's store, anxious to learn all that had been done. Ree Kingdom received a large share of the praise for the return of the stolen horses. Captain Bowen was delighted over his behavior and would not listen to one word about the lost pistol.

"I'll drive over that way an' pick it up along the road somewheres in the mornin'," he said. "An' to-morrow night I want you to come an' try some o' the new cider. You come too, son," he added, turning to John.

The boys thanked him heartily, for well they might esteem it a great favor and an honor to receive this invitation from the warlike old veteran. Again they inquired for the latest news of Jim Huson, and learning that he was likely to recover, set out for their homes.

"I have a presentiment that we shall see Big Pete again," said Ree thoughtfully.

"Are you afraid of him?" John quietly asked.

"No, I am not afraid of him, yet I would rather we should never meet again. But I think he will go west and though it is a big country, we might find him there. By the way, John, Capt. Bowen is just the man to give us advice about our expedition. Meet me about sundown at the old place. We will have a lot to talk about as we are on the way to make our call."

A few minutes later the boys separated. John going to the overcrowded little house of his parents; Ree to the Henry Catesby farm, which was the only home he had known since childhood. As he crept into bed in his attic room, and stretched his full length restfully on the straw-filled tick, again there came to him a vision of an unmarked grave in the quiet burying-ground, bringing an influence of sadness to all his thoughts.

"Oh, mother, my memory of you is the dearest thing in life," he softly whispered to himself, and his mind turned fondly to his childhood. Faintly he remembered his father. More vividly he recalled the coming of a neighbor with the news of his father's death—killed by Gen. Howe's troops as they advanced on Philadelphia, after succeeding in defeating the American soldiers at Wilmington, because Gen. Washington was misled by false information.

Poor Ree! How well did he remember his mother's grief, though he was too young to understand—too care-free to grieve long or deeply himself. Many times he had heard the story in after days, how his father and two companions were fired upon as they were hurrying forward to give notice of the enemy's coming; and one of the three being wounded, his father would not leave him, though in trying to save him, his own life was sacrificed. It was the third man, who escaped, who spread the news of the bravery and death of the elder Return Kingdom.

Ree did not know how long a time had elapsed, but it seemed a very little while after this sad story reached his mother that she removed with him to a newer part of Connecticut, where she earned a living for them both by weaving and spinning. A happy year or two slipped by and then—ah, well, he remembered the dreary day when some neighbors had taken him to see her whom he loved so well, buried beneath the elm trees, and he knew he was left alone.

Memory of the bitter tears he shed came freshly to the boy as he recalled it all— how, in but a few days, he was "bound out" to Henry Catesby with the promise that he should have a home and want for nothing.

Had he been in want? Oh, he had been supplied with food and clothing and a roof over his head. Could he ask more? Yes, a thousand times, yes! He wanted friends, companionship, love. He remembered no one who had cared for him in those early days, except—Mary Catesby, his hard master's little daughter. And she was still but a child when she was told to have no association with the "bound boy;" learning of which, he had steeled his proud young heart and had spoken to her only when necessary.

So with work, day in and day out, save for a few winter weeks in school, the years had passed, until he made the acquaintance of John Jerome, the son of a distant neighbor. Too poverty-distressed to be proud, he had known little happiness except a sort of sad pleasure he found in visiting the church-yard, where in summer he placed great bunches of wild flowers on the mound to him most sacred.

For two years he and John had been intimate friends. The latter being sometimes employed by Mr. Catesby, gave the boys additional opportunities of being with one another. Late at night after a long, hard day in the harvest fields, they had gone swimming together. They had borrowed a gun, and John's money bought the ammunition they used in learning to shoot, to practice which they had risen before sunrise; for at Old Sol's first peep the day's work must be begun. Many a time they had labored all day, then tramped the woods all night, hunting 'coons, coming home in time only to catch a wink of sleep before jumping into their clothes and away to work again.

Sometimes in winter when, by reason of John helping him with his work, Ree was able to secure a half-day off, the boys had sought other game, and shared the profits arising from their hunting and trapping. What with the knowledge they thus picked up themselves, and the instruction given them by Peter Piper and others, there were no two boys in Connecticut better versed in woodcraft.

Ree thought of all these things as he lay awake looking out through his window at the stars in the western sky. And as his thoughts ran on, he reflected on the death of Mr. Catesby a short eight months ago, and the great change it had brought into his life. From the moment Mrs. Catesby had called him to go for the doctor when her husband was taken ill, she had depended on him in nearly everything. It was he who took charge of all the farm work of the spring and summer, and the neighbors had said the Catesby place never produced better crops. With scarcely a pause except on Sundays, he had toiled early and late to accomplish this. Only within the past few weeks when the rush of the harvest was over, had he allowed himself any time for recreation. Yet it had been a happy summer, he thought. Mrs. Catesby, appreciative of his splendid services, had been all kindness; Mary Catesby had been agreeable as his own sister might have been. Both had forgotten, or at least no longer observed, the bar of social inequality which Mr. Catesby had set up against the "bound boy."

Then in August had come Mrs. Catesby's decision to remove to the city that her daughter might have educational advantages. It was with genuine regret that Ree had learned her plans. He would never have admitted even to himself that he had, in a certain boyish, vague way, dreamed of a dim, distant time when he and Mary might be more than friends; but maybe some such thought had been in his mind at some time. Strange it would be had nothing of the kind occurred to him.

Thus as he lay awake still pondering on the past, the present and the future, in the depths of Ree's heart of hearts there may have been a wish that he should become a successful man, wealthy perhaps, well-to-do certainly; but in any event, looked up to and respected.

But, oh!—What obstacles confronted him! How could he ever be more than a rough, uneducated "bound boy" that he was! The subject was not a pleasant one, but he gave it most serious thought, and determined for the hundredth time, that, come what might, he would make the most of his opportunities and ever be able to hold up his head in any company.

So his reflections passed to the future. He was to receive $100 for his summer's work. He also had some money which he had secured in odd sums from time to time, safely put away in the chest beneath his bed.

John Jerome had a hoard of savings, too. How should they best invest their joint capital for their proposed journey to the western wilderness, where, they planned, they would make homes and secure farms for themselves amid savages and wild beasts! They must be obtaining this and other information at once. They would have learned much that very evening had not the man to whom they were going in quest of advice, been assaulted by Big Pete Ellis. And what of that burly giant, by the way?

"But this will never do. I must be getting to sleep," Ree said to himself.

Going to sleep just when one wishes, however, is not always easy. Ree found it the very opposite. Tired as he was, his mind went over the adventure of the night, and in a round-about way to his future home in the wilderness, again, before his eyes closed. At last dreams came to him, and in one of them he saw Big Pete waving a white handkerchief as a flag of truce. He could not make out for whom the sign of peace was meant; for a war party of Indians seemed to be hot on the giant's trail, and it was in the opposite direction that Pete waved the handkerchief.

Ree recalled the dream when pulling on his boots in the morning, and pondered over the possibility of its having some significance.

Many times during that day the young man had occasion to remember the incidents of the night preceding. Everyone he met, it seemed, had heard of his adventure with Big Pete and they all congratulated him. More than one, too, warned him against the giant Ellis, saying the fellow would surely seek revenge.

Ree gave but little heed to this talk. Big Pete had had the chance to kill him, or at least to attempt it, and had not done so, evidently wishing to avoid blood-shed. But Peter Piper came along during the afternoon with a story which he had heard in the adjacent village, that gave the boy some uneasiness. Big Pete had sent word by a farmer he had seen at daybreak, that he would return to his old haunts and that not a man would dare to touch him; that he would not be driven off, though he had killed both Jim Huson and Marvel Rice, and that those who had interfered with him would suffer for it.

"He's a braggart," said Ree contemptuously.

"Jes' what he says, he will do. He's bad, bad, bad," said Peter Piper in his simple, earnest way.

So Ree came to look upon the matter with much seriousness. Somehow it occurred to him that the giant might seek revenge by burning the barn or poisoning the horses, or some such cowardly thing—he knew not what. For himself he was not afraid, and it is not strange that in the wildest flights of his lively fancy he did not for a moment imagine under what startling circumstances he was destined to next behold the fugitive criminal.

CHAPTER III.

The Beginning of a Perilous Journey.

"Hitch yer cheers up t' the blaze; it's a cool night fer September," said Captain Bowen, drawing his own splint-bottom chair toward the great fire-place of his homely but thoroughly comfortable home, and slowly sipping new cider, just old enough to sparkle, from the bright pewter mug containing it.

"An' help yerselves to some more cider, naow dew; I like a man to feel at home," he went on as Return Kingdom and John Jerome gave heed to his kindly bidding.

"Naow as I was a sayin'," Captain Bowen continued, "I r'ally kent advise yeu youngsters t' undertake these plans yer minds air set on. The Injuns hev hated us whites worse than ever sence the British turned their back to 'em after the war was over, an' comin' so soon after their hevin' helped the pestiferous Redcoats so much—they fit fer 'em tooth an' toe-nail as the sayin' is, ye know—as I was sayin' it rankles in their in'ards. General Washington—peace to him—he's did all he kin toward pacifyin' 'em, an' it ain't no wonder they call him the 'Great Father'; but so many other men hev cheated 'em, an' so many settlers air crowdin' into their huntin' graounds thet they air jist ready to lift the hair of any white man they catch sight on, a'most. Ye air takin' long chances, boys, I do tell ye."

"We want to hear both sides of the matter," Ree answered, and Captain Bowen resumed, saying in his own slow, homely but kindly way, that it was into the very thick of the savages that the boys were planning to go. He reminded them of the barbarous cruelties the Indians had practiced as allies of the King's troops in the war, and told them briefly the story of the battle Col. Crawford had fought with the savages in the Ohio country, ending with the burning of Col. Crawford at the stake.

He cautioned his young friends further of the hazardous nature of the journey through an unsettled country, a long part of the way lying over the Allegheny mountains. He told them of the cutthroats they would be likely to encounter—rough men, who, for adventure's sake, had gone into the war, and had never been satisfied to settle down to lives of peace and respectability after the close of the Revolution. As he paused at last, there was quiet for a minute or two. Then Return Kingdom said:

"We have thought of these things, Captain, and maybe we are head-strong, but we are bent on going. There is little future for a young man here. I will soon have no home, and John can well be spared from his. All we can do, if we do not emigrate and secure homes of our own, is to hire out as farm hands, and, as you know, labor is not greatly in demand. And as we have said, we expect to go among the Indians partly as traders. The land we shall settle upon, we expect to buy from them.

"Traders who have behaved themselves have not had much trouble, and we hope to make peace with every tribe we fall in with. The truth is, Captain, we really have more fear of finding ourselves in the woods with a lot of stuff we do not need, taking up the room in our cart and adding to our load, while that which we should have will not be within reach, than we have of trouble with the Indians."

"People say it will be only a few years until all the country about the Ohio river will be settled," put in John Jerome.

"Y-a-as, land agents say that," smiled Captain Bowen, "but I ain't so sure on it. Folks kin still find plenty of hardships right here in Connecticut 'thout pokin' off t' the Ohio Valley or the northwest kentry. But I tell you what, youngsters," he exclaimed with sudden enthusiasm, "I wish I was ten years younger, I'd go with ye, bless me if I wouldn't! They do bring tales of a marvelous kentry from the valley where my ol' friend General Putnam an' his colony settled!"

From that moment Ree and John had smooth sailing so far as getting advice and information from Captain Bowen was concerned. Then and there, however, the Captain had to tell them all he knew about the colony of brave men who had founded Marietta on the Ohio river, nearly three years earlier. "An' they do tell that game is thick there as fleas on a homeless, yaller dog," he said.

Though he knew that his wish that he might accompany the boys could never be gratified, Captain Bowen entered into the spirit of their plans and hopes with whole-souled ardor. He took great delight in telling the boys of his own youth and his adventures. He seemed to grow young again in their presence. Many times, too, he told them of sixteen-year-old Jervis Cutler, who, as a member of General Putnam's party, was the first to leap ashore and the first to cut down a tree in the new country whose settlement their enterprise had started.

Throughout, the boys found Captain Bowen's assistance of the greatest value. He went to town with them and helped them make their purchases, which he took into his own home, as a central point of assembling, the articles bought for the expedition, and helped to pack them in the handiest and most compact manner; and many a thing of value and use which he paid for with his own money, found its way at his hands into the outfit the lads were getting together.

The route of the journey Captain Bowen also aided the boys in planning, and his knowledge of the country stood them in excellent stead. He prepared maps for them—home-made affairs it is true, and not absolutely accurate, but yet worth much to those who planned to cross a thinly settled country to the wilderness beyond. It was by the way of Braddock's road that he advised the boys to go, following for the most part the course Gen. Putnam's party had taken after leaving Hartford in 1788. This party had made the trip in three months, including a long wait while boats were built in which to float down the Ohio river.

Captain Bowen figured that Ree and John could make better time and reach Fort Pitt (Pittsburg) before November first. There they could probably secure passage down the river without difficulty. In many other ways the genial old man lent his aid, and the boys never went to him that they did not find him brimming over with ideas for their benefit.

The news that Ree and John were going to the Ohio wilderness, and alone—soon spread through the surrounding country. Men who hitherto had scarcely noticed them, now came up to shake hands and advise the lads as to this or that, whenever they chanced to meet them. Others shook their heads gloomily and lost no opportunity to throw cold water on the project. The young people of the community talked more of Ree Kingdom and John Jerome going west than of anything else. There were envious ones who predicted that the boys would return a great deal faster than they went, or that they would not live to return at all. There were those of better dispositions, however, who, while recognizing the peril of the proposed venture, hoped and promised for the chums, all success.

It was with one of the former that John had an encounter which was talked about for weeks afterward. Jason Hard, the cobbler, a stocky Englishman, thirty years old perhaps, had been making slighting remarks about both John and Ree and their plans in the presence of a small company of men who were at the tavern awaiting the coming of the stage. As John approached the inn someone said:

"Now here's young Jerome himself, just say to his face what you were saying behind his back, Jason Hard!"

"I was sayin' that if his father wasn't shiftless, the young 'un wouldn't need to be leavin' 'ome, an' I say it again," ejaculated the cobbler, with arms akimbo, standing directly in front of John in an insolent manner.

"Look here! Take that back, you son of a Tory; my father has worked too hard to help his son get a start in life, for me to stand by and hear such talk! I say, take it back!" John bristled up like a porcupine.

The insolent Englishman sprang toward him as though to strike him, paused a moment, then suddenly let fly a blow straight for the boy's jaw. Most luckily John dodged in time, then with the agility of a cat he jumped toward the fellow and planted one fist just below his ear and the other squarely on his chin tumbling him to the ground.

Captain Bowen, who drove up just in time to see the encounter, was tickled amazingly. Others enjoyed the exhibition almost as much, and gave a cheer for the boy, while the badly bruised cobbler stood by rubbing his head, as though he wondered what had occurred.

Captain Bowen cautioned John against being too prone to take offense, especially as he would soon have Indians to deal with, but he secretly rejoiced in the lad's spunk. The Captain drove out of his way to take John home in his light wagon, while he was thus advising him.

The day of their separation was drawing quickly nearer, and John was spending as much time with his parents, brothers and sisters as he conveniently could. Often they urged him to abandon his preparations, but as it was with Return Kingdom that he was going, neither the father nor mother was willing to say he must not go. Both felt that he would be in good hands and in good company.

And Mrs. Catesby and Mary more than once, also, sought to dissuade Ree from emigrating. It was kind of them and their words of sympathy did Ree good, but he smiled at their fears and promised that he would return to assist in welcoming them home from the city, if they should be returning when Mary's education was completed.

How often Ree had cause to remember these promises so light-heartedly made, and the comforts he was leaving behind, within a few short months—when days of danger and sleepless nights of peril came!

There was so much to be done that time passed quickly. The Sunday preceding the Monday morning on which they were to start, Ree and John went to church together, and heard the good old preacher make special reference to them in his prayer—that God would guide and protect the young wayfarers and that they would not forget His mercy and wisdom. Every eye in the church was turned toward the boys, embarrassing them more than a little and making them wish they were safely started and well away from their excellent but altogether too curious friends.

Ree went home to dinner with John, and on his way to the Catesby farm in the evening he went across the fields to the quiet church-yard. Under the clear, cold stars he sat beside a grassy mound and for an hour was quiet as the grave itself. Many tender memories crept through his heart and in his thoughts was an unspoken prayer. Thus he took leave of the spot to him most sacred—his angel mother's grave.

To his surprise Ree found Mrs. Catesby and Mary waiting for him in the combined sitting-room and kitchen, when he entered the house.

"As you will be leaving so very early, sir, we thought to say good-bye to you to-night," said Mary with feigned solemnity. And a little later she said as they were talking, "I do hope you will be as good as your name and will bring your scalp safely home with you when you do 'return'."

Ree laughed and promised he would do so, but he blushed, and seeing which, Mary Catesby did the same, and looked her very prettiest.

"We shall think of you often, Return, and maybe you will be able sometimes to send us a letter. We shall be glad to hear from you, and oh, my boy, be careful—careful in all things," Mrs. Catesby said.

There were more teasing words from Mary, and more advice and real tears, from Mrs. Catesby and her daughter, too, before the final good-byes were said at last.

* * * * *

The late September sun spread a soft, warm haze over old Connecticut. A great, two-wheeled, canvas-covered cart lumbered slowly along the country road. Walking beside the one large horse which drew the vehicle, was Return Kingdom, his battered beaver hat on the back of his head, a smile of buoyant hope upon his lips. Sitting on a chest, his feet hanging over the front of the wagon box, his back against a bundle of blankets which made a fine cushion, was John Jerome. Joy in living and satisfaction with himself and all mankind were written in every line of his face. It was eight o'clock of a Monday morning. Two hours earlier the long journey toward the unknown Northwest had begun.

"Why, ye'r in a terrible hurry, youngsters! Thought I'd never ketch ye!"

It was Captain Bowen who called out, driving his spirited team alongside of the emigrant wagon as he did so.

"After ye'd gone, it come to me all of a sudden that ye'd stand a chance of meetin' an old friend of mine. He is an Iroquois Injun of the Mohawk tribe an' his name is High Horse. General Putnam gave him this knife fer doin' some thin' or other one time, an' High Horse gave it to me 'cause I shared powder an' bullets with him when he was out, an' durin' the war at that. Seems t' me naow, tew, that I pulled him through some sick spell or somethin'. Any haow he give me the knife. If ye see him tell him ye know me. I heerd that he was livin' up some crick emptyin' into the Ohio."

Almost before the boys could thank the Captain he had turned and was gone, having thrown a long-bladed knife with a curiously carved ivory handle—a relic of some Dutch trader perhaps—to Ree.

"I say! Maybe ye didn't hear as haow Jim Huson was able to git about t'day! Ye'll be hungry enough fer news I was thinkin', before ye air back agin!"

John waved his old cap and Ree shouted their thanks again, but if Captain Bowen heard he gave no heed; at least he did not look back.

At noon a halt was made at the roadside, close to a running brook, while the horse was fed and watered and the boys ate their lunch. They would not have exchanged places with a prince, now that they felt themselves fairly launched upon their long-talked-of enterprise. Their hopes were unblemished by any unhappy circumstance and the fine weather was as a tonic to their already lively spirits. They carefully examined their goods and wagon to see that all was in proper order before starting on, resolving to be attentive to every detail and let no mishap come to them through carelessness. On the road, too, they exercised care, remembering that a steady gait and not too fast, was necessary. And so the first day of their journey was passed most pleasantly.

For the novelty of it the boys camped out the first night, beneath a clump of beech trees, and no two young men ever more fully enjoyed a campfire's cheerful blaze.

Another and another day passed. It was in the afternoon of the fourth day of the journey that John stopped whistling "Yankee Doodle" to inquire of his companion who was taking his turn riding on the box:

"Ree, do you know much about this Eagle tavern where we are to stop to-night? I just happened to remember a story that was told in war time, that the house was haunted."

"Haunted by Redcoat spies, I guess," Ree answered. "The whole kit of them there at that time were the worst kind of Tories at heart, I have heard folks say, and Captain Bowen said something about it, too, you remember? But I guess they are all right now—got on the right side of the fence after the war was over."

"I don't mind Indians or wild animals—fact is, I'm just hankering to kill a bear, but I don't want anything to do with spooks or witches or anything of that sort," returned John. "I'll keep my eyes wide open for ghosts and robbers if we stay at the Eagle, at any rate."

"There is probably more reason to be afraid of bed-bugs," laughed Ree. "I don't believe the Eagle is so very bad a place or Captain Bowen would not have marked it as a stopping place. There was a man robbed and murdered there, it is true; but that was years ago, and needn't worry us."

So with talk of their journey and the progress they hoped to make in view of the necessity of reaching the wilderness before winter set in severely, the lads whiled away the time. It was nearly sundown when, passing through a woods which skirted both sides of the road, they found the Eagle tavern in view.

"See any spooks about?" asked Ree with a smile.

"No," said John quite seriously, "but I did see a mighty wicked looking man peeking out of the window of the barn across the road from the tavern there, just now. He seemed to be wanting to find out who we were and what sort of an outfit we had, without being seen by us. Without joking, Ree, I tell you I don't like it!"

CHAPTER IV.

The Man Under the Bed.

The Eagle tavern was a long, low structure and stood close beside the highway, on the opposite side of which was the weather-beaten log and frame barn to which John had referred. Near the tavern was a well and an old-fashioned sweep towering above it. At the roadside there was a moss-covered log trough at which horses were watered. An air of loneliness, such as is noticed about old, deserted houses, whose door-yards have grown up to rank weeds and briars, hung over the tavern, and the deep shadows cast by the setting sun heightened this effect. Little wonder is it that a feeling of depression came over the young travelers as they approached.

No other houses were near the tavern and guests were evidently few. The road which passed it was not a main thoroughfare, and no stage-coach made the Eagle a regular stopping-place. It may have been a handsome; much-frequented place at one time, but those days had long since departed.

Up to the watering-trough Ree drove, however, and unreined the horse, that it might drink.

"It does look kind of creepy around here," he remarked in an undertone; "but put on a bold front, John, we are going to stay, just to prove to ourselves that we are not afraid."

"I would a great deal rather camp out," John frankly confessed, "but you are the captain, Ree. I can stand it if you can."

A skulking fellow of about thirty years, none the handsomer for having lost nearly all his front teeth, came to help put up their horse when the boys had made their wants known inside the tavern. No unusual thing occurred, however, and the young travelers had shaken off the gloomy feelings which the lonely place inspired by the time their supper was ready. As they were by themselves at the table, a man whom Ree had not seen before approached and took a chair nearby, tilting back against the wall and calmly surveying them.

John kicked Ree's shins under the table. It was not, perhaps, a polite way of imparting the information that this was the fellow he had seen peering out of the barn, but Ree understood perfectly.

Having eyed the boys for a minute or two, the stranger said, in a gruff, indifferent tone:

"Good evenin'."

"Good evening, sir," spoke Ree, and John's voice repeated the words like an echo.

"Traveled far?" growled the stranger.

"Far enough for one day," Ree answered, little inclined to engage in conversation with the man, for the fellow's appearance was far from favorable. The sneaking glance of his eyes, his unshaved face and uncouth dress, half civilized, half barbarian, gave him an air of lawlessness, though except for these things he might have been considered handsome.

For a minute the stranger did not speak, and John suppressed a laugh as he saw with what cool unconcern Ree returned the fellow's stare whenever he looked at them.

"Don't show off your smartness, bub," sharply spoke the man at last, as he fully comprehended that Ree had purposely given him an evasive answer, "I asked a civil enough question."

"And got a civil answer," Ree quickly replied.

"I see you are emigrating," the stranger went on, trying to make his coarse voice sound friendly. "I just had in mind puttin' a flea in your ear. Because it is the wrong time of year to be goin' west, in the first place, and the woods are full of

Indians and the roads alive with cutthroats, in the second place. If I was you young shavers I'd sell out and wait a year or two, or till next spring anyhow, before goin' any further. I s'pose you have a lot of goods in your cart; goin' to do some tradin' with the Mingoes, maybe."

John pricked up his ears at this reference to the nature of their cart's contents, but waited for Ree to speak. This the latter did at once, respectfully but firmly.

"We are much obliged for your advice and the interest you take in us, but we expect to be able to take care of ourselves both on the road and in the woods. Aren't you the man we saw in the barn as we were coming up?"

The question was an experimental thrust. Ree wished to learn whether the fellow would give a reason for having spied upon them. The man looked at him searchingly before replying.

"I never clapped eyes on you till you come into this room," he coolly said, however. "What do you take me for? I was only goin' to tell you that I know a man that will buy your outfit if you want to sell!"

"Which we do not," said Ree with moderate emphasis.

"You would find a little ready money mighty handy; I don't s'pose you have any too much," the stranger replied with assumed carelessness.

"Say; tell us what you are trying to get at, will you!" John spoke up, with a show of spirit.

"Hold your horses, sonny!" the fellow growled. "You are almost too big for your breeches!"

"Well what do you take us for! Maybe you have some more questions to ask!" John exclaimed, and Ree smiled to see how heated he had become.

The stranger relapsed into silence, and presently arose and strolled away.

Having finished their supper, the boys went into the general sitting-room of the tavern, a long room in one end of which there was a bar, and sat down by themselves to talk. As their conversation flagged, Ree drew from his belt beneath his coat, the ivory handled knife Captain Bowen had been at such pains to give them. In an idle, listless way he began stropping the blade on his boot-leg.

A tall, lank man of fifty, with a thin, sharp face and nose, whom the lads had noticed sitting opposite them, reading a pamphlet of some kind, came nearer and seemed to take an unusual interest in the sharpening of the knife. His keen eyes watched every movement the blade made. Coming close up, he quietly said:

"If that ar ain't Cap. Bowen's knife over to Bruceville, he hes the mate to it! His'n is the only knife I ever see with a handle like that."

"Do you know Captain Bowen?" asked Ree, and as the man said he did, and told them who he was, both lads held out their hands which the newcomer shook cordially. It was like meeting someone from home; for the lanky individual was a peddler who had often visited at Captain Bowen's house and knew many of their friends.

As they talked further the peddler said, sinking his voice to an undertone, "I want yeow youngsters to hev some advice; it won't cost ye nothin', an' it may save ye a heap of trouble. There's a bad 'un stayin' at this old tavern, an' he's likely to want yeow boys to pay fer his rum. Naow, he won't ask ye fer money, but be all-fired keerful that he don't git it from ye anyhow. Jes sleep with one eye open, an' hev a hick'ry club handy t' yer bed."

Ree told the peddler of their conversation with the stranger at the table, and as he described the fellow, their new friend said:

"He ar the one, an' him an' the hos'ler here are bad 'uns."

As the hour grew late Ree and John went to the barn to see that their cart and horse had been properly cared for, and returning, went immediately to bed. For half an hour they lay awake talking of their journey. Their money was between them in the big four-poster and each had a pistol within reach. At last they said "Good night" to one another, and settling themselves in comfortable positions, composed themselves to sleep.

All had grown quiet about the old tavern. The ticking of the big clock down stairs, and the baying of a hound off in the woods somewhere, were the only sounds which reached the ears of the young emigrants. And thus they forgot their travels and where they were, and the danger which hovered near.

It was sometime after midnight when Ree was suddenly awakened. He had heard no sound, nor could he tell what had disturbed his slumber; but he had instantly found himself, eyes wide open, every sense alert. Without the slightest noise or movement he lay listening. A minute later he felt for just an instant the touch of something cold against his skin.

"A snake," was his first thought, and a little thrill of horror crossed him as the idea of a reptile being in their bed, flashed over his brain. Again he felt the touch, cold and clammy against his side; and, intending to grab the serpent, if such it was, and hurl it from the bed, with a quick movement of his arm he made a desperate grab. He caught and for but an instant held a human hand, large and coarse.

"John!" Ree spoke the name with startled emphasis, and its owner rose up in bed like a flash.

"What? What is it?"

"There is some one in this room! He has been reaching into the bed, trying to rob us."

As he spoke Ree sprang out upon the floor. "And here's the window open! That shows where he came in. Get your pistol and be ready to fire if he tries to jump out. I am going to skirmish for the rascal!"

Faint rays of moonlight made the room not entirely dark, but Ree could see no sign of the intruder as he stepped softly to the middle of the floor. It was a useless action; for, as he was between the three dark walls and the window in the outer wall, the robber could easily see him without being seen himself. It was a fault of Return Kingdom's that he did not properly consider his own safety, and the wonder is that he did not in this instance become the target for a bullet.

"I'd better yell for help," suggested John.

"You'd better not!" said Ree emphatically, peering into the dark corners. "I cannot be mistaken, but if I should be—well we don't care to be laughed at."

Not a sound was heard as both boys remained perfectly quiet. Then on tip-toe Ree went to all the corners of the room, his left hand outstretched before him while his right held a pistol ready for instant use.

"John, did you sneeze?" he demanded as a smothered "kerchoo" came from the direction of his friend.

"He's under the bed, Ree! He's under the bed! Call help!" This was John's answer and his tone was sharp with excitement.

In a trice Ree was at the foot of the bed and looking beneath it. A dark object there moved slightly.

"Come out of that!" Ree sternly demanded, and the click of his pistol as he cocked the weapon sounded loud and clear. At the same moment the object beneath the four-poster began to crawl and soon coming forth, stood erect—the stranger the boys had met at supper.

"Oh, it's you, is it?" ejaculated Ree with an inflection of contempt in his voice; but the next instant the intruder's hands were about his throat.

"Help! Help!" yelled John Jerome.

Finding the young man he had seized, a much harder problem than he was prepared to handle, and frightened by John's cries, the stranger gave Ree a shove and sprang toward the window.

"Help! Robbers!" yelled John again, and now the stranger had one leg out of the window. But he got no further. Ree seized him about the body; the robber seized him in turn, and his foot striking the ladder by which he had climbed up, it went tumbling to the ground. With a frightful oath the fellow endeavored to throw Ree after it. For a second they both balanced on the window sill at the very verge of falling. Then John seized the robber's hair, and dealt him a blow with the butt of his pistol. He raised the weapon to strike again, but Ree had now secured his release from the villain's grasp and fired at him just as the fellow plunged to the ground, leaving a bunch of his black hair quivering in John's hand.

The bullet took effect, for the boys found blood on the ground beneath the window next morning; but the robber dashed around a corner out of range at such speed that there was no opportunity to fire a second time.

A pounding on the door told the youthful travelers that the house had been aroused, and they lost no time in admitting the landlord, accompanied by the greatly excited peddler.

"What's all the row about?" demanded the tavern-keeper, holding a lighted candle over his shoulder.

"I want to investigate before I say what it is all about," Ree answered, emphasizing the "all."

"A pretty sort of a place, this is!" put in John indignantly. "We might have been murdered in our beds!"

"How can I help it, boy? Just you keep your breeches on!"

"I'll have to put them on first," John ejaculated, and forthwith proceeded to do so.

Ree took the landlord's candle and turned back the bed clothing. He found the leather wallet containing their money, undisturbed, but as he picked it up, he noticed a hole in the sheets and tick of the bed.

"Look, here," he exclaimed, "here is where the row you complain of, began. The man who has just gone out of the window, evidently crawled under the bed and having cut a hole through the tick, reached for our wallet. His cold hand on my bare skin waked me up. The question is, how did he know where the money was?"

"The skunk!" exclaimed the peddler, eyeing the tavern-keeper sharply.

"How should I know anything about it?" the landlord hotly responded. "I ain't responsible for there being robbers about, am I?"

Ree had joined John in the task of dressing, while the proprietor of the establishment sat on the bed, the least concerned of any, over what had taken place.

"Haow should yeow know anythin' about it?" cried the peddler suddenly turning toward the man. "Why, yeow ain't even asked who the thief was! Yeow wouldn't 'a come up stairs if I hadn't 'most dragged ye! It looks consarned strange, that's what I say! An' yeow settin' there like a stick, sayin', 'Haow kin I help it!'"

The landlord winced and squirmed, and was glad enough to hurry down stairs when Ree said authoritatively: "Now let's have no further talk about this matter, but get our breakfasts at once, if you please. It will soon be daylight."

"Ree Kingdom, you make me mad!" cried John Jerome, as the landlord disappeared. "Why didn't you let me crack that old villain on the head? If I didn't know that you are the only one here who has kept cool, I'd be mad in earnest. If any of our goods have been disturbed, I'll show the old Tory!"

Ree smiled at his friend's blustering tone, but the peddler slapped him on the back and told him he was a "reg-lar man-o'-war with flags a-flyin'."

The gray glimmer of dawn was in sight as the boys crossed the road to the barn and by the light of the tallow candle in the old-time lantern, inspected their cart and horse. All was secure. Recognizing his young masters by the fine instinct some animals have, Jerry, their horse, whinnied loudly, as though saying he was all right but ready to move as soon as convenient. Hay and grain were given the faithful animal, and the boys went in to their own breakfast.

The meal of potatoes and bacon was soon disposed of, the peddler sitting at the table with them. He was going in their direction for a mile or two and would accompany the lads, he said.

"We'll be glad to have you," Ree answered.

"Whatever Ree Kingdom says, I say—only he always gets the words out first," said John. "I am like the old trapper who came hurrying up to General Washington saying he could lick all the Redcoats on earth with one hand tied behind his back. But the war was all over then, though he did not know it, and so he didn't get a chance to try. He meant well, you see, but was a little behind hand."

"That's a pert yarn," smiled the peddler, "an' there ain't nobody gladder than I be tew see yeow so chipper; but I swan, lads, I only hope ye'll be as jolly as ye be naow, come six months—I only hope ye will be!"

CHAPTER V.

A Mysterious Shot in the Darkness.

"I am going to keep my eyes open for that cut-throat that was under the bed. There's no telling what he might not do," said John with quiet determination, to Ree, when the peddler had left them and they were fairly under way for the journey of another day.

"I have thought of that," Ree answered, "and you see I have put the rifles where they will be handy. There is no use of carrying them, I guess, but the time is coming when they must always be within reach."

The peddler had accompanied the boys to a cross-roads a couple of miles from the Eagle tavern, enlivening them with many odd tales of his experiences. Now they were alone again, and as the country through which they passed became rougher and wilder, the lads realized more fully than ever that theirs was a serious undertaking.

Yet they were happy. The trees were putting on bright colors; the air was fragrant with the odor of autumn vegetation. The water in every stream they crossed was fresh and clear, and fall rains had made green the woodland clearings. Quail called musically from time to time, and once the "Kee-kee-keow-kee-kee" of a wild turkey was heard.

At noon, beside a dashing brook which tumbled itself over a stony bed as though in glee with its own noisiness, the travelers halted. They unhitched Jerry that he might graze, and kindled a fire to boil some eggs. These with brown bread, a generous supply of which Mrs. Catesby had given them, and ginger cake which Mary Catesby had announced she had made with her own hands, made a meal which anyone might have relished. To the boys, their appetites sharpened by the fine air, every morsel they put between their lips seemed delicious.

"We won't long have such fare," they reminded one another.

"We will have venison three times a day though," said John.

"Yes, we will have so much meat we will be good and tired of it; because we must be saving of our meal this winter, and until our own corn grows," Ree answered thoughtfully.

"Well, don't be so melancholy about it, Old Sobersides," cried John. "Why, for my part, I could just yell for the joy of it when I think how snug we will be in our cabin this winter! And what a fine time we are going to have choosing a location and building our log house!"

"That, as I have so often said," Ree answered, "is the one thing about our whole venture that I do not like. We will be 'squatters.' We won't own the land we settle upon except that we shall have bought it of the Indians; and that is a deed which the government will not recognize. But we will have to take our chances of making our title good when the time comes, though we may have to pay a second time to the men or company, or whoever secures from the government the territory where we shall be. Or we might settle near enough to General Putnam's colony to be able to buy land of them. We must wait and see what is best to do."

"Ree," said John, earnestly, "I know you are right; you always are. But I don't like to think of those things—only of the hunting and trapping and fixing up our place, and eating wild turkey and other good things before our big fire-place in winter—and all that. You see we will have to sort of balance each other. You furnish the brains, and I'll do the work."

"Oh that sounds grand, but—" Ree laughed and left the sentence unfinished.

When, by the sun, their only time-piece, the boys judged they had been an hour and a half in camp, they resumed their journey. They had secured so early a start that morning, that they had no doubt they would reach the Three Corners, the next stopping-place designated on Captain Bowen's map, before night; and indeed it lacked a half hour of sundown when they drove up to the homely but pleasant tavern at that point. It was so different a place from the Eagle tavern that the boys had no fear when they went to bed, that the unpleasant experience of the night before would be repeated.

Several days followed unmarked by any special incident, except that the lads were delayed and a part of their goods badly shaken up by their cart upsetting into a little gully. Fortunately, however, little damage was done.

At the end of two weeks so thinly settled a country had been reached that nearly every night was spent in camp. Yet these were not disagreeable nor was there much danger. Only one man who answered the general description of a "cut-throat" had been seen, and he seemed inclined to make little trouble. He rode out on a jet black horse from a barn, near which a house had at one time stood, its site still marked by charred logs and a chimney. Perhaps it had been burned in the war-time; at any rate the place had a forsaken, disagreeable appearance, and the rough-looking stranger emerging suddenly from the barn, put the young emigrants on their guard at once.

For two hours the man rode in company with the boys, and finding out who they were, proposed to spend the night with them. Ree would have permitted it, but by his actions John so plainly gave the fellow to understand what he thought of him, that the stranger at last rode back in the direction he had come, cursing John for the opinions which the latter had expressed. The boys slept with "one eye open" that night.

Daily the road became worse and worse. For great distances it was bordered on both sides by forests and the country was rough and broken. There were wild animals and, undoubtedly, Indians not far away, but the settlements were yet too near for the young travelers to have much fear. So when their camp fire had burned low in the evening, they piled on large sticks of wood, put their feet to the blaze, and, wrapped in their blankets, slept splendidly. One night when it rained—and the water came down in torrents—they made their bed inside the cart; but if the weather was pleasant they preferred to be beside the glowing coals.

An adventure which had an important bearing on the future, befell the boys early in the fourth week of their travels. They had resolved to be saving of their ammunition, and wasted no powder in killing game for which they had no use, though they twice saw wild turkeys and once a bear, as they left civilization farther and farther behind. But when provisions from home began to run low, it happened, as so often it does, that when they felt the need of game to replenish their larder they chanced upon scarcely any.

"One of us must go through the woods, keeping in line with the road, and shoot something or other this afternoon," said Ree, at dinner one day. "The other will not be far away when he returns to the road again."

"Which?" John smiled.

"I don't care. You go this time and I will try my luck another day," Ree answered. "Get a couple of turkeys, if you can, old boy; or, if you can get a deer, the weather is cool and the meat will keep."

So John set off, planning to work his way into the woods gradually and then follow the general direction of the road and come out upon it sometime before sunset. He waved his hand to Ree, a smile on his happy freckled face as he disappeared amid the timber.

Slowly old Jerry plodded on; slowly the miles slipped to the rear; slowly the time passed. Ree thought of many things during the afternoon and planned how he and John should spend the winter hunting and trapping and secure, he hoped, a large quantity of furs. Two chests they had were filled with goods for trade with the Indians, also, and they would receive skins in return. These would add greatly to the store they themselves accumulated, and they should realize a considerable sum when they came to market them. Ree hoped so. It was no part of his plan to go into the forest fastnesses merely to hunt and trap and lead a rough life. No, indeed! He wished to make a home, to grow up with the country and "be somebody."

Lower and lower the sun sank behind the darkness of the trees which seemed to rise skyward in the western horizon, and as the early October twilight approached, Ree began to watch for John's coming. He had listened from time to time but had heard no gun discharged, and he laughed to himself as he thought what John's chagrin would be if he were obliged to come into camp empty-handed. And when Old Sol, slipped out of sight and his chum had not appeared, he inwardly commented: "You went farther into the woods than was good for you, my boy! I suspect I have already left you a good ways behind."

So he drove to a little knoll beneath an old oak, and unhitched. He kindled a fire, then busied himself straightening up some of the boxes and bundles which had slipped from position during the day, often stopping to look back along the trail in hope of seeing John; and when the darkness had become so dense he could see but a few rods from the camp-fire and still his chum was missing, alarm invaded Ree's thoughts. He could not imagine what detained the boy. But he toasted some bread and broiled some bacon for his supper.

A sense of loneliness over his solitary meal added to Ree's anxiety, because of John's non-appearance, and presently he walked back along the road a considerable distance, whistling the call they had adopted years before. The darkness gave every object an unnatural, lifelike look; bushes and tree trunks assumed fantastic shapes. No human habitation was within miles of the spot, and as the echoes of the whistling died away and no answer came, Ree was almost frightened. Not for himself but on John's account was he conscious of a gloomy foreboding in all his thoughts. What should he do if the boy had fallen a victim of some bear, perhaps, or lawless men.

Slowly he retraced his steps to the campfire's light. Weighing the whole question carefully, however, as to whether he had not better go in search of his friend, he decided he could do no wiser thing than to remain where he was until daylight; then if John had not arrived, he would set out to find him.

Piling more wood on the fire that the light might help to guide John to camp, the lonely boy wrapped a blanket about his shoulders and sat down, resolved to remain awake to watch and listen. He heard only the soughing wind and old Jerry nibbling the short grass nearby, and the hooting of an owl in the forest gloom. Thus an hour passed, and then suddenly a sound of soft footsteps broke upon the boy's ear. Was it John slipping up stealthily to try to scare him? Ree thought it was, but in another instant he detected the foot-falls of more than one person, and sprang to his feet.

"How!" The word was spoken in a deep guttural tone almost before Ree had time to face about. At the same moment he saw two Indians stalking toward him.

"Howdy!" Ree promptly answered, though filled with misgiving; for at a glance he saw that the savages were fully armed. One was of middle age, tall and stately as a king. The other was much younger. As they came within reach Ree held out his hand, but the Indian either did not see or refused to accept the proffered greeting.

Nevertheless Ree spread a blanket near the fire and asked the savages to sit down. They made no reply. The older of them looked at him intently and gazed around in evident surprise to see the lad alone. The younger stepped around the fire and looked inquiringly into the cart.

"I am just a trader," said Ree, with an open frankness in his tones which even a savage must have appreciated. "There are two of us, but my partner went hunting and has not yet come back. Sit down, brothers; I have no fresh meat to offer you, but my friend will soon return with some, I hope."

The elder Indian seated himself saying: "White men steal, Indians no steal."

"There are good Indians and good white men," answered Ree, but he was keeping an eye on the younger savage, who seemed to have found something in the cart which interested him, for he slyly put his hand inside.

"Oh, do be seated!" Ree exclaimed as he noticed this. There was irony in his voice which made the older Indian shrug his shoulders, but the young white man led the Indian brave, a chap but little older than himself, away from the cart. With some force he drew the buck to a blanket and motioned to him to sit down.

Appearing to give the matter no further thought, Ree placed bacon before the Indians saying simply "Eat." They drew out their knives and cut and broiled each a slice of the meat. This they ate, and it was rather remarkable that they did so, for Ree well knew that the Redskins had no relish for food which had been freely salted. He therefore judged their eating to be a sign of friendliness, and seated himself quietly by the fire.

"White man go far—goes to Ohio? Yes—long way—far—far. Snow comes; hurry fast," said the older Indian.

"Yes," said Ree, guessing at the speaker's meaning. "We have a long way to go, and must be in our cabin before deep snow comes."

"Delaware country—much game," the Indian was saying, Ree having told him whither they were bound, when suddenly a rifle cracked behind them and a bullet whistled past Ree's ear. The young Indian at the opposite side of the fire, gasped and fell backward.

Seizing his rifle, Ree instantly sprang away from the firelight. The elder redskin did likewise and just as quickly.

Who could have fired the shot? Ree trembled with dread that it had been John. All was quiet save for the night wind rustling the leaves and branches overhead. There came no sound to indicate whose hand had sped the bullet from out of the forest gloom.

A minute passed. It seemed like ten, to Return Kingdom, and, forgetting prudence, he stepped from behind the cart's protection, full into the campfire's ruddy glow, making of himself an easy target. He bent over the wounded Indian and found the blood flowing from a wound in the young brave's neck. Quickly he tied his handkerchief about the injury, then bathed the fellow's forehead and temples with water from the bucket he had filled at supper time. The older Indian crept up to watch this operation, but did not come fully within the lighted circle.

"Who fired that shot, my friend?" Ree asked, very earnestly.

"White men steal," the Indian answered, and shook his head.

It was evident then that the savage suspected some white person of having made this attack with intent to commit robbery. Ree hoped this was the truth of the matter but there was a terrible suspicion growing in his mind that his own friend and partner, through some awful mistake, had fired upon the Indian. He drew the wounded man to the rear of the cart and placed him on a blanket beyond the campfire's light. The other savage made no move to help him, but crouched in the darkness intently listening, watching.

Of a sudden the Indian's rifle flew like a flash to his shoulder. At the same instant Ree heard John Jerome's familiar whistle, and springing forward, seized the red man's weapon in time to prevent the speeding of a leaden messenger of death to his friend's heart. He answered John's call as he did this, praying and hoping that it could not—must not, have been his friend who had fired the shot which would probably end the younger Indian's life.

CHAPTER VI.

On Lonely Mountain Roads.

"What's happened, Ree?"

The tone in which John asked the question, satisfied Kingdom that his friend knew nothing of the shooting. Better than this, however, it satisfied the Indian who knelt silently nearby, still listening, that the boy he had so nearly shot, knew nothing of the person who had fired from the darkness.

Quietly, but in tones the Indian could hear, Ree related what he knew of the mysterious occurrence.

"Who could it have been, Chief!" John asked, turning to the Redskin and addressing him with the easy familiarity he used toward every one.

The Indian shook his head. "Paleface," he grunted at last; "no tried to kill Indian; tried to kill white brother there. Black Eagle thinks long and knows how bullet flew. Man-that-shoots-from-the-dark wishes much to steal."

Black Eagle's theory was far from satisfying Ree, but the Indian's manner persuaded the boy that the redskin at least knew nothing of the attack himself. Yet both boys knew the necessity of keeping a sharp eye turned in all directions. They could not tell positively as yet whether the Indians were friends or foes, nor at what moment an attack might be made by a hidden enemy.

"What kept you, John? I was worried," Ree said in an undertone, yet taking care that Black Eagle should hear, lest the savage should suspect him of plotting. But before John could answer, the red man, bending low, darted away in the darkness.

"What's the old chap up to?" asked John, startled by the Indian's sudden movement.

"I think he is only scouting around to see what he can discover; but keep your eyes and ears open, it has been mighty ticklish around here to-night."

As they watched and listened, John told of his afternoon's experience. He had gone a long way into the woods without seeing any such game as he wished, and had about decided to content himself with some squirrels, and return to the road, when he came upon a deer-lick—a pool of salt or brackish water, in a flat, level place, to which deer and other animals came to drink, or to lick the earth at the water's edge to satisfy the craving which all animals have for salt. As it was then nearly sundown he determined to hide nearby, confident he would get a shot at a deer as soon as darkness came. Concealing himself in some brush at the north side of the lick, the wind being from the south, he waited.

Scarcely had the sun set when a fine young doe approached the brackish pool. One shot from his rifle brought the pretty animal down, and in a few more minutes he had secured the skin and best portions of the meat. Slinging these over his shoulder, he set out to find the road and Ree's camp-fire. But he had been careless in keeping his bearings, and walked a long way in the wrong direction. When he did find the road at last, he knew not which way to go to find the camp. He secured a light, however, by flashing powder in his gun, and thus found the tracks of old Jerry and the cart. He then knew which way to go, but traveled a couple of miles before coming within sight of the camp-fire.

He heard a rifle shot but paid little attention to it, and saw nothing of any prowler, though he came up in the direction from which the mysterious attack was made. When Ree called to him, he had dropped the venison and it still lay at the roadside a hundred yards from camp.

"We must have an understanding with one another that when either of us leaves camp, he shall return at a given time unless something happens to prevent it," said Ree; "then the other will know that something has happened and can act accordingly. I was probably not more than a mile away when you found that deer-lick. If you had let me know, it would have saved a lot of worry on my part. Why, I was just on the point of going in search of you. And as it was, old boy, you whistled just in time. That Indian heard you coming before I did, and a little more—"

"And he would have sent me to Kingdom come," said John, finishing the sentence, very soberly. "Your watchfulness saved me, and I can't—"

"You better get your venison into camp," Ree whispered, interrupting John's thanks, "I'll crawl over and see how that young Indian's getting along—poor chap."

The wounded Redskin was conscious as Ree bent over him.

"Don't speak if it will hurt you, but if you can, tell me who fired that shot at you," Ree urged.

"Black Eagle come soon," was the buck's only answer; and indeed it was but a few minutes until the other Indian returned. Ree met him and inquired calmly. "What luck, Black Eagle?"

"Gone. Paleface robber gone."

"Who was it? Where has he gone?"

"Gone," the savage repeated.

"Turn in and get some sleep, John; Black Eagle and I will watch a while," said Ree.

"Gone," growled the Indian with gruff dignity; and wrapped himself in a blanket and was soon asleep.

John likewise lay down, but Ree, resolving to exercise every care, remained awake through the whole night. Twice John awoke and wanted to take a turn at guard duty but each time he was told to go back and "Cover up his head." Reluctantly he did so. He felt that he would do anything in his power for Ree Kingdom, but he was far from guessing what Fate had in store for him to do in his friend's behalf before they should see Connecticut again.

With the first light of morning Ree went reconnoitering hoping to find the trail of the young Indian's mysterious assailant. Scarcely had he started when Black Eagle joined him, and in the road three hundred paces from the camp they came upon the trail together. A single man had approached the camp on foot—a white man it was certain, for he wore boots—and from behind a thick thorn bush had fired the shot. Then the trail led back along the road, but soon disappeared in the woods.

"If North Wind die, scalp will hang here," said Black Eagle, pointing to his belt. "Black Eagle follows trail long—even many moons, but he will get the paleface scalp."

What to do Ree did not quite know. He disliked to lose time in helping the Indian to find the man who had shot his son, yet disliked to leave the wounded North Wind without doing something for him.

"White brothers go far; go now," said Black Eagle as they returned to the camp. "Go long way off and never mind. North Wind stays with Black Eagle," the Indian added.

Ree made no objection to this arrangement. Reaching camp they found that John had some venison steaks ready. The young Indian arose and greeted Ree by silently shaking his hand. It was plain to be seen that he was suffering greatly, but he said nothing and when the breakfast was ready he tried to eat.

Thankful that the night of watching was past, Ree and John prepared to pursue their journey. They watered Jerry at the little brook hard by and hitched him to the cart. When they were ready, Ree took a knife from their stock of goods and gave it to Black Eagle, who with North Wind stood looking on, saying:

"Maybe we will never meet again, but here is a present which we wish you to keep. We do not know the enemy who fired upon us, but we were in danger together and whether it was your foe or ours, who attacked us, we would have fought together. Good-bye."

"We journey to the fires of the Mohawks," Black Eagle answered. "North Wind now goes forward but Black Eagle, his father, follows the trail of snake which shoots from the dark."

As he spoke the Indian turned and strode away. North Wind followed, Ree's handkerchief still about his neck. He was really too sick to travel, but it is a severe wound, indeed, which makes an Indian unable to move when necessity demands it.

For a moment the young travelers looked after the red men; then a word to their horse and they were once more upon their way.

It was a glorious morning. Particles of frost glistened on the leaves and grass and in the road; a light wind set the trees and brushes rustling, a rabbit went bouncing across the path, and still neither boy spoke as they tramped along beside the cart, Ree in advance, driving.

"Who fired that shot?" John asked at last, as though speaking to himself.

"May as well ask old Jerry, or the wind," Ree answered. "The same question has been on my mind so long I am trying to think of something else."

"But I can't help wondering," John persisted, "if it could have been the lone horseman we saw the other day. Could it have been Big Pete Ellis, trying to kill you, Ree? I have been expecting to meet that fellow."

"We must keep our eyes about us," was the only reply.

Several days passed and the mystery of the shot from the darkness was still unsolved. The boys had now reached the mountainous country and the nights were often cold. The days, too, gave promise of winter's coming, and had it not been that they were hopeful of Indian summer weather in November the young travelers would have been discouraged. Their progress had not been so rapid as they had planned. The roads were too bad to permit fast traveling. In many places they were little better than paths through the woods, and though there were stretches of smoother going, occasionally, there were other spots in which fallen trees or other obstructions blocked the way.

Old Jerry stood the strain of the journey well, and that was certainly a consolation; for some of their friends back in Connecticut had told the boys they had better stay at home, than attempt to make the trip with only one horse. Often, too, it was the case that the lads drove far out of their course to pass around great obstacles, and they eventually found that they had gone miles out of their true course. Many were the hardships they encountered, and one adventure which they had must be related here.

For days at a time no human being was met on those lonely mountain trails and it was this fact which gave rise to much uneasiness when John one day, for just a moment caught sight of a rough-appearing fellow in their rear. He had gone back along the road to search for a bolt which was lost from the cart box, when he chanced to look up and saw the strange fellow a quarter of a mile away, coming toward him. The man raised his rifle and sprang in among some trees as he caught sight of John, his movement being so quick that the boy did not get a good look at him, and neither in going on beyond the spot where the fellow had been, nor in returning after he had found the lost bolt, did John see him again.

"We must be on the watch-out constantly," said Ree when told of the incident. "I would have thought nothing of it, but for the man's desire to hide."

"That is what I can't understand," said John, and as he thought the matter over it added to a downcast feeling which had seized upon him. It was by his looks more than by words that he betrayed his low-spirited condition, then, and at other times, as day after day nothing save the trees, great rocks and wooded hills and frowning mountain sides were seen.

On the other hand, Ree's quiet disposition seemed almost to disappear in the face of hardships and difficult obstacles. If the cart broke down he whistled "Yankee Doodle," while he managed to mend it. If the road was especially rough and their progress most unpleasantly slow, he was certain to sing. Even Jerry could not fail to catch the spirit of his cheerfulness no matter what bad luck they had, and from looking glum, John would change to light-heartedness every time. Ree's smile was a never failing remedy for his blues.

"Time enough to be blue and all put out when you have utterly failed," Ree exclaimed one day. "And if you only make up your mind to it, it is the simplest thing in the world not to fail. If I were the general of an army, I wouldn't own up that I was whipped as long as I had a breath left. Now just suppose that Washington had given up at Valley Forge!"

"Well, I want to say that the chap who starts out west thinking he is going on a frolic, will be mighty badly fooled," John answered. "I am learning, but it is like the Indian who believed powder didn't amount to much unless it was in a gun; so he filled his pipe with it. He learned a heap."

"Ho, ho, pardners both!"

The voice came so suddenly to the young travelers, they started and looked around questioningly. With a flying leap from some brush which bordered the road, came an odd looking woodsman.

"Lift my ha'r if ye ain't the nearest bein' kittens of anythin' I've clapped my old goggles on in the emygrant line in all my born days!" Putting his hands to his sides the stranger laughed uproariously.

"Oh, it's funny, ain't it!" exclaimed John Jerome, witheringly.

"Age is not always a sign of wisdom," said Ree Kingdom in much the same tone.

"Right ye be, lad; right ye be," said the woodsman, quieting himself. "But I swan I'm that glad to see ye so young an' bloomin', both, that it jes does me old eyes good. Where ye bound fer, anyhow?"

The speaker was tall and rugged, his age probably fifty years. A grizzled beard clustered round his face and his unkempt hair hung almost to his shoulders. On his head was a ragged coon-skin cap. All his dress was made of skin or furs, in the crudest frontier fashion. He was not a disagreeable appearing person, nevertheless, for his eyes twinkled merrily as a boy's. Each in his own way, Ree and John noted these facts.

"I might say that we are going till we stop and that we came from where we started," said John in answer to the stranger's inquiry.

"What a peart kitten ye be!" smiled the man, looking at him quizzically.

"To be honest with you, we are going to the Ohio country," said Ree Kingdom, satisfied that the stranger wished to be friendly.

"Ye've got spunk, I swan!" the fellow exclaimed. "Don't let me be keepin' ye though; drive along, we kin swap talk as we're movin'."

"How far do you call it to old Fort Pitt?" asked Ree.

"Well, it ain't so fer as a bird kin fly, an' its ferder than ye want to walk in a day. If ye have good luck ye'll come on to Braddock's road afore supper time, an' if ye don't have good luck, there's no tellin' when ye'll get thar. It want such a great ways from here that Braddock had his bad luck. If he hadn't had it—if he'd done as George Washington wanted him to, he'd 'a' got along like grease on a hot skillet, same as you youngsters."

"Hear that John? We will make Fort Pitt in a day or two," cried Ree.

"Yaas, it was forty odd years ago that Braddock had his bad luck when he bumped into a lot of Injuns in ambush. I was jest a chunk of a boy then, but I've hearn tell on it, many's the time, by my old gran'sire who learned me how to shoot. I was a reg'lar wonder with a gun when I was your age, kittens. I've picked up some since then though! See the knot-hole in that beech way over yonder? Waal, I'm going to put a bullet in the middle of it."

Taking aim, the stranger fired. "Ye'll find the bullet squar' in the center," he said, in a boastful way.

"Shucks!" exclaimed John, who was often too outspoken for his own good. He raised his rifle and fired. "There's another bullet right beside your own, mister," he said.

"Well I swan! So there is!" called out the woodsman in great surprise. "But I'll bet a coon-skin my tother kitten can't do the like."

Like a flash Ree's rifle flew to his shoulder and he seemed to take no aim whatever; yet the bullet flew true. But just an instant after he fired the crack of another rifle sounded behind him. A leaden ball shrieked close to his head and a lock of his hair fell fluttering to the ground.

CHAPTER VII.

On Into the Wilderness.

Great as the shock of the sudden attack and his narrow escape was, Ree gave only a little yell of surprise and anger, and ran in the direction from which the shot had come, drawing his pistol as he went. He found no one. Though utterly regardless of the danger he might be in by thus exposing himself, he made a careful search.

"Land o' livin', boy, ye'll be meat for the redskins before ye've crossed the frontier, if ye don't be keerful!" cried the woodsman, quickly coming up, springing from tree to tree, and thus always keeping their protecting trunks between himself and the point from which the mysterious shot had been fired. "What is the varmint pepperin' away at ye so, for?"

"I haven't the least idea, for I don't know who it is," Ree answered.

But he was glad the woodsman's frank manner left no room to suspect him of treachery, although there had been grounds for this suspicion in the circumstance of the shot having been fired just as his own rifle and that of his friend had been discharged.

John had remained on guard beside Jerry and the cart, watchful for any sign of their strange enemy, completely mystified by the attack. Presently he joined Ree and the hunter who were searching for the trail of the would-be assassin. Tracks were found at last (high up on the rocky hillside)—those of a white man, for he wore boots; but they were very faint and Ree declared he would waste no time in attempting to follow them.

"But I do believe, John," he said, "that the shot which wounded North Wind was intended for me, and the fellow who shot, then, fired again to-day."

"You are thinking of Big Pete; I know you are!" John answered. "But I am sure you are mistaken, Ree. Why it was miles and miles away that North Wind was shot, and there hasn't been a day since then but what we could have both been killed, perhaps, by some one hidden along the road."

The woodsman, when he had heard the story, coincided with John's opinion and Ree said nothing more, though he was not convinced that he was wrong.

The brisk talk of the stranger turned the boys' thoughts to other subjects as the journey was resumed. He was by no means a disagreeable fellow. His real name was "Thomas Trout," he said, but he was everywhere known as "Tom Fish." He had tramped over all the hills and valleys for miles around and seemed to know the country thoroughly. He accepted the boys' invitation to eat dinner with them, and gave a share of the pounded parched corn he carried in a pouch at his belt, in return for venison and coarse corn bread, John having baked the latter on a flat stone beside their camp-fire, the previous night.

When in the afternoon, Tom Fish left the boys he told them they would be like-ly to see him at Fort Pitt, and gave them many directions as to where they had better "put up" while at Pittsburgh, as he called the place, such being its new name at that time.

John declared he would not sleep a wink that night, but remain on guard until morning. "For we must be prudent," he said, in a very sober tone, which from him sounded so funny that Ree laughed outright.

And yet John was probably as prudent a boy as Ree; for the latter was so almost entirely fearless that he rushed into danger in a way not prudent at all, and many severe lessons which he learned afterward did not make him cautious as he should have been.

The night passed without one disturbing incident and the rising sun found the boys on their way once more; before its setting they reached Pittsburg.

"Fort Pitt," as they were accustomed to call the straggling hamlet, stood at the foot of the hills at the confluence of the Allegheny and Monongahela rivers. Because of its location it was an important place and even at the time of which this is written (1790) was a point much frequented by traders, trappers and hunters.

It was with a feeling of awe, that Ree and John drove into the town, and noticed its old fort, its brick and log buildings and general air of pioneer hospitality. People stared at them, and some called to them in the familiar way of the border; but everyone was good-natured and helpful and almost before the boys knew it their horse had been unhitched and fed and they themselves were eating supper in a long, low brick building which served as a sort of public house.

From the first it had been the young travelers' intention to sell their horse and cart at Fort Pitt and secure passage for themselves and goods on some flat-boat going down the river. They spoke of the settlement which General Putnam and others had made at a place they called Marietta (still known by that name) as their destination, and gave a general idea of their plans to the men who talked with them as they gathered about the big fire-place in the evening. They found they would probably be able to secure transportation down the Ohio within a few days, in company with a party of emigrants who had been building boats for the trip, expecting to go to Kentucky.

When the young travelers started out next morning to find a purchaser for old Jerry, however, they discovered that at that time of year, the demand for such property was far from brisk. As they walked along the main street or road, they chanced upon Tom Fish, who hailed them in his rough, but happy way, and they told him just how they were situated.

"Don't sell the nag, then; come right along with me. I'll show you the way into a country full of Injuns and game enough to suit ye, in short order; an' ye won't have to pay no passage down river. Why, there's jes the spot ye're lookin' for west o' here—rivers an' little lakes, an' fish an' game—no end o' game. Good place for tradin' too; Injun towns every forty rods or so."

The woodsman then went on to tell the boys that several years earlier, a fort, known as Fort Laurens, had been erected on the Tuscarawas river, in the woods beyond Pittsburg. He was planning to go in that direction, for a purpose he did not state, and would willingly act as guide. He cautioned the boys, however, that there was little sign of a broken road for them to travel upon and that Fort Laurens had long been abandoned because of the hostility of the savages. But the confidence of the young traders that they could make friends with the Indians, and Tom's glowing accounts of the country of which he spoke, caused them to look with favor upon his proposition.

"We will think about this matter," said Ree, "and let you know. You will be here a day or two?"

"Yaas, a day or two," said Tom Fish. "But don't let me influence ye; it's mighty reesky business you kittens is bent on."

"It seems to me like a good plan," Ree reflected aloud, when he and John were alone. "If we went to General Putnam's settlement we would still feel that we must go up the Muskingum river to reach the Indians and profitable trading, and would have to build a raft or buy a boat to carry our goods. Moreover, people here say that within a few years the country all about Pittsburg will be settled up and that land will become valuable."

"Whatever you say suits me," said John with a laugh; and then and there Ree gave him a talking to for being so ready to accept the judgment of another, instead of having thoughts and opinions of his own.

But one or two ridiculously low offers the boys received for their horse and cart, and the discovery that they could not find room on the boat down the Ohio except at a fancy price, resulted in their decision to join Tom Fish. They talked all day of the subject, but when they went to bed that night, they knew that not for many months to come would they sleep again within the borders of civilization.

A frosty November morning ushered in another day, and early as they were astir Ree and John found the little town wide awake. Tom Fish was sky-larking all about saying good-bye to friends, and just a little under the influence of whiskey. It seemed that everybody knew him; and people having found out from Tom what they had not already found out from others, about the venturesome lads from Connecticut, quite an assemblage gathered to wish the travelers good luck.

A repeated suggestion which had been made to the boys was that they should abandon their cart and take with them only such goods as they could carry by using old Jerry as a pack-horse. It was true that for a portion of the distance they proposed to travel, there was a rough road, but beyond Fort McIntosh, at the mouth of the Beaver river, they would have no road but the rough Indian trail. But Tom Fish said he "reckoned old Colonel Boquet's road was still there," and that they should take the cart; and they did so.

Tom had joined the boys as their clumsy vehicle creaked along a muddy street, a little more serious than usual, because of some news he had heard, he said, but boastful as ever.

"I was talkin' to a big seven-footer in the tavern last night," he said—"A feller that had a grudge ag'in' me once. He never liked me till I threw him over a house one day;—threw him clean over a house. It makes me larff!"

John laughed, too, at this, but he said: "Tom Fish, you weigh a good three stone (forty-two) more than I do, but I believe I could throw you in a wrestle. When we stop for dinner, I am going to put you on your back!"

A laugh long and loud came from the woodsman's throat. "Why, what a playful kitten ye be!" he exclaimed. "Why, I could toss ye up in the air and ketch ye nigh a dozen times whilst ye were only thinkin' of throwin' me."

"I'd like to see you try it," cried John.

"Put aside your nonsense, you two, until noon, now do," Ree laughingly urged, "and tell us, Tom, of that Colonel Boquet whose road we are to follow."

"Waal, that's quite a yarn," said Tom Fish. "But le' me see now; le' me see. It was back when I was jes a young buck, 'long 'bout '64, that this Colonel Boquet, who was a mighty decent citizen for a Frenchman, made up his mind to get a whack at the pesky Injuns which had been killin' an' scalpin' an' burnin' an' robbin' all along the border of Pennsylvania an' Virginia an' Lord knows where all.

"Waal, the state of Pennsylvania an' the state of Virginia helped him with sojers an' he mustered scouts enough so that in all he had nigh onto 2,000 men. He marched 'em straight into the woods, the whole caboodle on 'em, clearin' a road as he went, an' takin' along a lot o' sheep an' cows, and provender for the sojers without end. He went straight along till he come to the Muskingum river, an' there he camped out, makin' a show with all his men an' pack-horses an' everything, that scared the Mingoes an' the Delawares half to death for fear he'd stay right there an' build a town amongst 'em.

"They was willin' to do most anything to get rid of him, an' there was only one thing that he would hear to. He give 'em jes' ten days to trot into his camp every prisoner they had in all their towns far an' near, an' told 'em that if ary a one was held back, he'd march on every pesky village an' knock 'em sky high an' burn 'em down.

"Waal! them Injuns was so scared, they commenced gettin' their prisoners together right off, and they trotted two hundred on 'em up to the front door of Colonel

Boquet's tent inside them ten days. An' there was doin's for sartin then!—Pow wows among the sojers who found all sorts of relations that the Delawares or the Wyandots or the pesky Mingoes had carried off, an' pow wows among the men, an' the women an' the children that was brought out o' their captivity like the Children of Israel.

"Then Colonel Boquet marched 'em all back to Fort Pitt an' he sent for me an' told me what he'd done, an' asked me what I thought on it. I was scoutin' out of Fort Pitt then, and I jes' shook his hand an' says: 'Colonel Boquet ye're a reg'lar rip-snorter.'"

"Did you ever hear of the terrible Captain Archer, the outlaw of war times?" asked the fun-loving John, inventing the name to see what Tom would say; for he had his own opinion as to Colonel Boquet having asked Thomas Fish what he thought of that Indian expedition.

"Cap. Archer? Old Cap. Archer! Well I rayther guess I knew him, an' if he ain't forgot it, he carries a little lead pill out of my old steel bottle of Injun medicine, clean to this day. Yaas, many a scrimmage I had with old Cap. Archer."

John was for carrying his questioning further, though he could hardly keep from laughing, but Ree shook his head, unwilling to make fun of one who was so kind to them.

The travelers made excellent progress that morning, finding a very fair road for that rough country, along the river. They met occasional settlers and hunters and whether he knew them or not, Tom Fish always stopped to talk and always asked whether everything was quiet along the border. Many shook their heads, and spoke gloomily of the outlook for peace with the Indians remaining long unbroken.

From a couple of friendly Indians they met, Ree secured a quarter of venison in exchange for a cheap trinket, and although he accompanied the performance with a great deal of bragging, Tom did show the boys that he was a past-master in the art of broiling venison steaks. The fine dinner they had as a result, set his tongue wagging more than ever, however, and John Jerome was more than anxious to take some of the vanity out of him.

They had camped upon a hillside sloping down to the river—the Ohio. The day had come on bright and warm as Indian summer could be, and John had thrown off his coat.

"Now, Mr. Fish," he said with a laugh, "You see the river down there? I've been thinking there may be some one of the same name as yourself in that water, and I've a mind to send you to visit your relations."

The merry laugh of the hunter rang shrill and clear.

"Be ye? Oh, be ye?" he cried, jumping to his feet. "If it wa'n't fer hurtin' ye, I'd throw ye clean across to yon hillside!" and he pointed to a spot nearly a mile away, across the river.

"It's a good thing for you there are so many leaves on the ground to break your fall," John answered, rolling up his sleeves.

"Don't wrestle so much with your mouths," Ree admonished them.

"Why, I could handle both of ye; come on, the two of ye to onc't!" the hunter cried.

But the next moment he found in John, alone, about as much of a task as he cared to undertake. For two minutes they heaved and tugged, John's wiry frame seeming to be all around the woodsman, who was by no means clumsy, though he could not put him down. Then they broke apart and for a minute made feints at one another, each hoping to secure an advantage.

At last the hunter's arms shot out, his hands seized John's arms so quickly, and he lifted the boy off his feet and keeled him over with such dexterity, that the lad lay sprawling on his back almost before he knew what was happening.

The glee of Tom Fish was quite ridiculous. He danced about and almost screamed with laughter.

"It is your turn, Ree," said John good-naturedly.

"Whenever our friend is ready," Ree responded.

"Come on! Come on!" Tom cried. "Oh, what frisky kittens ye be!"

Peter Piper, the half-breed, had taught Return Kingdom a trick or two at wrestling. And now he allowed the hunter to lift him off the ground, then he let his muscles relax, his dead weight falling in his opponent's arms. Suddenly getting his feet to the ground in this way, he sprang against the hunter's muscular frame with such rapidity of thought and motion that he was able by a tremendous lightning-like effort to jerk one of the man's legs from under him, sending him down, while he, himself, came uppermost.

"Ye're pretty fair," Tom Fish muttered; but it was plain to be seen that something he very little expected had happened to him.

CHAPTER VIII.

Friends or Foes?

Tom Fish had a profound respect for Return Kingdom from the moment the latter threw him; but he was no less pleasant and agreeable than before, and he proved himself a valuable friend then and in days long afterward.

When night came, as the wind was blowing cold, Tom very deftly built a shelter of branches and small saplings. His way of bending two little trees down and fastening them together with their own branches, making of them the support of the "shack," was a method Ree and John had never seen used and was the secret of his being able to "build a house" in very little time.

It was very comfortable sitting before the fire, thus sheltered from the wind. Tom especially enjoyed it for his tongue ran on at a tremendous rate as he told stories of extraordinary adventures.

John urged him to tell more and more, and he might have gone on talking all night had not Ree admonished him and John that they must turn in promptly in order to make an early start in the morning. Wolves were howling not far away, and the plaintive but terrorizing cry of a panther could be heard in the distance, as the little party lay down to sleep. No doubt the young emigrants thought many times before dreams came to them, of what the depths of the wilderness must be, if the foreboding sounds which reached them were a fair example of what the outer edge of the forest fastnesses afforded; but they rested well and were early astir.

Crossing a fine, level country, though thickly grown with great trees, on this day, the boys saw plainly the evidences of the road made by the Boquet expedition. There were the stumps of big and little trees and the half-decayed remnants of the trees which had been cut down, on both sides of them. Although so many years had passed since Col. Boquet had made this trail, the work his men had done made the progress of the Connecticut boys and their hunter companion faster than it would otherwise have been, and three days passed rapidly without other adventure than the meeting of a small party of Indians who scowled and passed on, and the killing of a large panther by Ree, the animal having terribly frightened old Jerry by dropping from a tree squarely upon the faithful horse's back, one night.

On the fifth day after leaving Pittsburg the travelers crossed a high ridge and obtained a glorious view of the country toward which they were pressing on. In the distance rivers of water and great oceans of tree tops, deep valleys and wooded hillsides were seen.

"Ye ain't fer from the 'Promised Land,'" said Tom Fish, lightly, much less moved by the grandeur of nature's display than were the boys. Then he indicated the location of a point, far beyond and out of view, at which the old trail they were following, turned to the southwest and an Indian trail turned toward the northwest, leading on to the "Sandusky Plains" near Lake Erie.

It was apparent that Tom had settled in his own mind the locality in which the boys should erect their cabin and make their home. He had their interest at heart, the lads did not doubt, but they were unwilling to accept his judgment absolutely. It was arranged between them, therefore, that Ree should go ahead and spy out the lay of the land—and especially investigate the "lake country" of which Tom had so often spoken. If he should find it all that was represented, well and good; if not, they knew that along almost any of the rivers to the south and west of them, were fertile lands and Indian villages which would afford that which they sought—crops and trade.

And so on the morning of the fourth day after their having taken to the Indian trail toward the "Sandusky Plains," the matter having been explained to Tom Fish, Ree left his friends behind. It was a perilous undertaking upon which he set out. They had now reached a wild and rugged country whose hills and valleys almost swarmed with game. Deer, bears and wolves were abundant. Panthers, wildcats and smaller game were frequently seen, and Indians were all about, though the party had thus far met but few.

But Return Kingdom had no fear—that was something he did not then know. He was only anxious to quickly find the right place for their residence and to make no mistake in selecting it. A light snow had already fallen, making it desirable that he and John should get themselves settled without delay. This was his thought as he hurried on alone.

Under a big beech tree Ree camped at night, building no fire lest it draw unwelcome guests toward him, but wrapping his blanket about himself and sitting, not lying, on the ground, his rifle between his knees. Any one passing, even very near, would have supposed his dark figure to be that of an old stump, and he spent the night with a feeling of safety, not entirely comfortable in his position, but little disturbed by the snapping of twigs and the rustle of leaves which told that forest prowlers were near.

Crossing a river at a shallow place next day, Ree mounted a hill and climbed a tall hickory whose upper branches rose above all other trees near it.

The weather had become warm and pleasant again and he would be able, he knew, to obtain a fine view. Just what he expected to see, he had not thought, but the grandeur of the scene he beheld was magnificent. Far as he could see the ocean of nearly leafless treetops rose and fell in giant waves, broken here and there by lakes or rivers, he knew not which, glimpses of whose waters and bushy banks, he caught. Here were lowlands—there highlands, and through the latter he traced for a long distance the course of the river he had crossed earlier in the day. Ree drew out a chart he had obtained at Pittsburg.

"It must be the Cuyahoga river—or Cayuga as some call it—and I am right in the heart of the lake country," he whispered, as he steadied himself in the tree top. "We will build our cabin near the river."

Without more delay the boy climbed down and strode forward in the direction of a valley which he had seen two or three miles to westward. In time he came to a sloping hillside and looking beyond he saw a splendid stream of swiftly flowing water. At the foot of the hill was a narrow tract of about four acres almost bare of trees, though deep grass spoke of the soil's fertility. Rising above the river was a large knoll sloping down to the natural clearing.

With every sense delighted by the fine prospect, Ree ran down the hill, across the clearing and to the summit of the knoll or bluff. The ripple and splash of the river, the bright sunshine and his discovery of this ideal spot delighted him.

"The very place we are looking for!" he exclaimed aloud. "Here is grass for Jerry, a fine clearing for the beginning of a farm—wood—water— game—everything!"

Anxious to join his friends and tell them of this good fortune, Ree dashed down the bluff and ascended the wooded hillside opposite. Panting, he reached the summit and suddenly,—stopped.

As though they had been waiting for him, there stood watching him a party of Indians. They were dressed entirely in savage costume. Not one wore any garment of civilization as did many of the savages farther east. With stolid composure the Redskins looked at the boy, though they must have wondered what the young Paleface was doing, alone in the forest's depths.

Quickly recovering his presence of mind, Ree coolly stepped toward them, holding out his hand to one he supposed to be the chief, saying, "How, brothers?"

The Indian shook his hand but did not speak. The same second another Indian stepped up and seizing Ree's hat, put it on his own bare head. Another grabbed the boy's rifle, as though to take it from him.

Ree smiled, but he held firmly to his gun, and snatched his hat from the young brave who had seized it. One of the Indians now ordered that Ree be let alone. But this was not the one the boy had taken to be the chief, and Kingdom quickly perceived that he had made a rather serious mistake. But he nodded his thanks to the Redskin and explained, using signs when words would not do, that he was a trader and that his friends and store of goods were not far away.

It caused Ree some alarm, however, when at a signal from the chief the Indians gathered about in such a way as to hem him completely in. And this alarm was decidedly increased as he noticed at the chief's belt, a white man's scalp. There could be no mistaking it.

The savages made no move to molest the boy further than to prevent his leaving them, but gave him to understand that they believed him to be a spy. Seeing this the boy offered to conduct them to his friends and merchandise. To this they agreed after some parleying and placing Ree between two big, swarthy fellows, they set off in single file, suspicious, it may be, that he would lead them into an ambush.

Ree gave little thought to this. He knew that if John and Tom had made good progress that he could reach them by nightfall and the suspicions of the Indians would be allayed.

It was wonderful how easily the savages followed Ree's back trail, and they traveled at good speed. But hours passed and no sign of the wagon of which the lad had told them was found. The doubt of the Indians increased and they became ugly and impatient.

In vain Ree tried to explain that his friends must have been delayed, but he himself could not understand why no gleam of light, no smoke of their camp-fire, even, was visible as the day wore away, and soon he found that he was indeed a prisoner; for as the savages presently prepared to go into camp, their first act was to bind the white boy's hands behind him and tie his feet with strong ropes of bark.

A full sense of his danger came to Ree's thoughts, but he put on a bold front and emphatically objected to being tied, saying he had no thought of running away and that early the next day his statement that he was a trader would be found true.

The Indians gave no heed to his indignant words. They built a small fire by flashing sparks with flint and steel, and ate their supper consisting only of pounded parched corn and dried meat. This they shared with Ree, and though he ate heartily he was thinking of other things. Every time he looked across the fire he could see the gruesome scalp at the belt of the chief of the party. Little wonder that he became apprehensive for his safety. It would not do, however, he thought, to let the Indians see that he was worried, and he began to whistle. The savages gazed at him in wonder. Suddenly one young buck arose, stepped over to the boy and struck him viciously on the cheek.

His temper instantly fired, Ree shot out his feet, bound together though they were, striking the savage full in the stomach and sending him headlong, partly into the fire.

As a tremendous howl of rage arose, Ree forgot that he was bound—forgot that his better plan would have been to keep cool. He sprang up, breaking the strings of bark which tied him, with seeming ease, and, as the enraged Indian rushed toward him, he dodged the club the savage brandished, and landing a tremendous blow on the redman's neck with his fist, grabbed his rifle from the ground and sped away into the forest and the darkness.

With terrific yells the Indians took up the pursuit. On and on Ree dashed among the bushes and over brush and logs, springing wildly aside at times to save himself from dashing out his brains against a tree—hurrying fast and faster, he knew not whither, his pursuers crashing after him.

The pursued nearly always has the advantage over the pursuer. Ree found himself drawing slowly away from the Indians, who made so much noise themselves they could scarcely hear him, and suddenly halting, he crept softly away in another direction. Soon the savages went past, pell mell, certain that the boy was ahead of them, and the sounds of the chase died away.

Listening intently, to be ready for the slightest alarm, Ree turned to go back the way he came. It was difficult in the darkness to do this, but he believed that if he could return to the vicinity of the Indians' camp-fire he could easily get his bearings and travel without loss of time in the direction of his friends. The darkness seemed less intense now that he had become accustomed to it, but he must exercise every care. To step on a dry stick or to stumble and fall might be fatal—might mean his capture and death.

Fortune favored the brave lad, for presently the dim light of the smoldering camp-fire came into view. He paused a moment, then turned confidently in the direction in which he thought John and Tom Fish must be. He had not taken forty steps, however, when a dark figure loomed up suddenly before him, and with exceeding quickness and quietness glided behind a tree.

It was well indeed for Return Kingdom that his quick eye saw this movement. Turning again, he ran, but instantly the dark figure darted in pursuit. Discovering that he was in danger of being driven into the very arms of the Indians he had so recently eluded, Ree changed his tactics. Certain that but a single savage was behind him, he wheeled and ran toward the Indian at full speed.

They were not far apart. Before the Redskin had made out what the boy was doing, the latter had hurled himself upon him and thrown him to the ground.

Fiercely the savage struggled; with tremendous energy Ree retained the upper hold, his grip secure on his opponent's throat. Neither spoke. The Indian could not, and Ree had no wish to add to the noise made by their thrashing about among the leaves and dry twigs. He knew that he could kill the savage warrior but he dreaded to do that. It would mean trouble with the Indians for a long time to come, upsetting his most cherished plans. And yet his own life was in danger, and—he dared not relax his hold.

Yet something must be done, and quickly, for soon the other Indians would be returning, and more than this he could not hold out long against the greater strength of his red antagonist. Ree resolved, therefore, to make the Indian understand that he did not wish to kill him, then let go and take his chances in a foot race.

But at this instant, the Redskin, by a mighty effort raised himself partially upon his feet, secured the release of his right arm, on which Ree's knee had been, and clutched the boy's throat with a vise-like grip. Never had the venturesome Connecticut lad been so near death as he was at that moment. Steadily the Indian continued to gain the upper hand, and as he tightened his grasp on Ree's throat the boy's tongue seemed to be forced from his mouth.

Then it was that Return Kingdom's grim, unyielding determination which meant victory or death—a determination which, once formed, would have stopped for nothing though it swayed the earth, asserted itself. With the power of an unbending purpose, Ree raised to his feet, dragging the savage with him. He grasped the Indian's body and with strength most extraordinary, lifted him from the ground, then suddenly he cast him violently down as though the brave were a great stone which he wished to break.

Astonished, bruised, exhausted, the Indian lay as he had fallen. The whole struggle had occupied but a minute or two, but it had been furious. Both the combatants were panting like dogs. Now was Ree's opportunity. He stooped down, grasped the redman's hand and shook it gently.

"We should be brothers. I would not try to kill you," he spoke in a low, friendly way.

The Indian made no answer. Again Ree shook his hand, then picked up his rule and walked rapidly away. Looking back, he saw the savage rising to his feet and returning to the camp-fire. He was sure then that he had made a friend of an enemy. But he lost no time. There were but a few hours of darkness remaining to cover his escape while he searched for his friends, and with every sense alert he hastened on, though faint and weary from the violence of his exertions. He felt the necessity of finding and giving warning to John and Tom and the thought kept him going.

At last the morning came—slowly at first and then with a rush of light which set the crows a-cawing and wood-birds singing; and still the worn-out, lonesome boy looked in vain for his friends. But he wavered not for a moment, though ready to acknowledge himself completely lost, and thus, pressing on, he came soon after sunrise to the bank of a deep, wide ravine. He remembered having crossed it the day he left John and Tom, and soon he found a path leading down into the gully.

Assuring himself by careful scrutiny that the coast was clear, Ree pushed through the bushes and trotted down the bank's steep side; and in another moment came squarely upon the cart and the camp of his friends. But where were John and Tom? Consternation filled the lad as he wholly failed to find them, and as he also discovered that the camp-fire was no fire at all—only a heap of dead ashes. Where was old Jerry, too?

A great fear came into Ree's heart, which was increased a thousand fold, as in another moment he saw the faithful horse a few rods away—dead. There was a bullet hole in the gentle, patient animal's head.

CHAPTER IX.

The Scalp at Big Buffalo's Belt.

A great lump came in Ree's throat as he looked upon the body of honest old Jerry, and stood for a few seconds watching in a dazed, helpless way the big blue flies which buzzed about the lifeless animal in the morning sunlight. Then he saw for the first time that carion birds, buzzards, perhaps, had been feeding on the horse's flesh.

The oppressive silence and desolation of the camp were as dead weights on the lad's spirits, already burdened with most unhappy thoughts, and standing as still as the motionless trees about him, he could not summon back the resolution and courage which had kept him unfaltering throughout the night. The snapping of a twig recalled his scattered senses, however, and his sudden movement frightened a gaunt wolf which had crept up almost to the lifeless horse, and now went skulking away.

"I cannot understand—cannot think, I must get my wits to working, some way!" the boy exclaimed in a half whisper, "what in the world can have happened?"

Again Ree's mind gained the mastery over his fatigued body and his powerful determination seemed again to drive the weariness away. He stooped and stroked but once or twice the dead horse's damp foretop, then hastened to the cart. Nothing in it had been disturbed. He looked carefully about the shelter of poles and brush which had been built, and found everything in comparatively good order. Surely things would not be in this state if his friends had been driven off or killed by Indians. It must be that they were attacked, had repulsed the enemy and had now gone in pursuit.

But why had they not returned? There was no doubt but that old Jerry had been dead at least a day, and John and Tom would, in that case, have been absent nearly as long.

With feverish anxiety Ree searched for a trail which would show the direction taken by the enemy or his friends, or both, but the sound of a stealthy footstep on the bank above caused him to spring to the shelter of a tree.

As he watched and listened, he heard voices, and quietly stepped into the open; for he would have known John's tones among ten thousand. And at the same minute John and Tom Fish saw Ree gazing up at them, and both ran toward him, John crying excitedly: "Return Kingdom! Oh, but I am glad to see you!"

"Dutch rum an' fire-water, it's happy I am y'er back!" Tom Fish exclaimed.

"What has happened, John?" asked Ree in his usual quiet way, grasping his friend's hand.

"What ain't happened? It beats me as I ain't ever been beat yet," Tom Fish made answer.

"It was another of those mysterious shots, Ree—the very morning you left us," said John, putting his hand affectionately on his chum's arm.

"Another?" Ree spoke more to himself than to either John or Tom, and something made him think of Big Pete Ellis and the fellow's threats.

"It was the same sort of a shot as before, but in broad daylight," John answered. "We had just got the cart down into this gully and were preparing to get it up the other side, when we heard a rifle shot and—old Jerry fell dead. I saw the smoke curling out from the bushes just half a minute later, and Tom and I both ran back up the hill. But there was no one near. We did find a trail but it was mingled with the tracks of the horse and cart, and the snow being gone, we could not follow it. For miles around the woods seemed as quiet as a Sunday at home. We looked all about but—"

"Only one thing is plain, some Mingo or somebody has a grudge ag'in ye, or else there's been some consarned queer coincidences," broke in Tom Fish. "It beats me!"

"I don't see what we are to do, Ree! Tom and I decided just to wait here until you came back. But what have you been doing? Why, your hands and face are frightfully scratched, and you look all played out!"

"I guess I've had my hands full," said Ree with a sad little smile. "But tell me where you two were. Why is there no fire?"

"Such a time as we have had!" was John's sorrowful answer. "Poor old Jerry was scarcely dead before there were hawks or buzzards circling around above us, and when night came, wolves and other animals howled all around us, and so near we would have been afraid, had we not had a big fire. Toward morning it became quieter and I was asleep, and Tom on watch, when a bear came poking around."

"Biggest bear ye ever seen," interrupted Thomas Fish.

"Well," John went on, "we both set out after that bear, though it was pitch dark. We had a long chase for nothing, though, for we caught sight of the big fellow only once, and not long enough to get a shot at him. Coming back, it was light, and we stopped to explore the gully. But we did not expect to find you here, Ree. We would not have come back when we did, only to keep the buzzards away from the horse till we can burn the body. And I don't see what we are to do. But you haven't told a word about yourself."

Ree was busily thinking, and for a little time made no answer. Then Tom and John spoke again, asking where he had been and what he had found.

"Why, I'll tell you," he answered them. "I came upon a first-class place for a cabin, on a bluff right at the bank of a splendid little river, and a little natural clearing around it. About five minutes later I came upon some Delaware Indians and as they wouldn't believe me when I told them who I was, they made me a prisoner. I got away in the night, and here I am."

John's eyes opened wide, and excitedly he demanded to know all the particulars of Ree's adventure. Tom Fish whistled a long, low note and almost closing his eyes, he looked toward Ree with a squint which was more expressive of his astonishment and interest than words could have been.

As the three of them sat on the thills of the now useless cart, Ree told them more fully of his experiences. Many were John's outbursts of interest, and Tom whistled in his peculiar way more than once.

"Can't more than kill us, and we may as well die that way as starve to death," said the old hunter, as Ree spoke of the probability of the Indians soon finding their camp, and straightway he began preparations for breakfast. As they gathered about the savory meal which soon was ready, the conversation turned again to the mysterious attack which had ended the life of their horse.

John could not be persuaded that it was not some prowling Indian who had fired the shot, but Ree urged both him and Tom to be on their guard constantly and he would be the same, he said, for there was no knowing when another bullet might come whizzing toward them, nor when one of their own lives might not be thus snuffed out.

As breakfast was finished, John and Tom pleaded with Ree that he should lie down and get some rest, but he took a cold bath in the brook close by, instead, and would not listen to them further. All three were keeping their eyes open to detect the approach of Indians, for they did not doubt the savages would soon come, especially since the re-kindling of the fire had sent a stream of smoke steadily skyward, and now this signal of their whereabouts was made all the more plain by the building of a much larger fire upon and about the body of the unfortunate horse.

"Let them come," was the confident declaration of Return Kingdom, as Tom Fish had suggested that the savages could not be far away. "We will meet them as friends," he went on, "and I honestly believe that when they find that we are peaceable traders, there will be no trouble whatever."

Tom whistled and squinted as Ree took this bold stand, but he had learned that the boy "had a long head," and made no further remonstrance against the plan proposed.

About noon the savages arrived. John discovered a dark face peering out from some bushes on the bluff, and waved his hand in that direction in a friendly way. The searching eyes instantly disappeared. It required courage to follow the program Ree had mapped out, now when it was known that vengeful and cruel Delawares were lurking so near, themselves fully protected by the bank and brush, and trees; but when, a few minutes later Ree saw an Indian looking down at them, and the fellow put down his gun as a sign of friendliness, they knew they had acted wisely.

Notwithstanding the show of friendliness, however, Tom Fish said: "Keep your wits about ye, kittens, there ain't no snake in the woods as treacherous as them varmints."

Two savages were soon seen coming down the path, and Ree and John, laying down their guns, as the Indians had done, walked forward to meet them. Thus peace was secured for the time being, at least, and as the boys shook hands with the Redskins, the latter gave them to understand that their chief was in waiting to be met and conducted to the camp.

Ree went to the cart and secured from their stock of merchandise a small hand-mirror in a round, pewter frame with a pewter lid over it, and with this for a present to the chief, he and John were guided to a spot not far away where the savage warrior and his braves were assembled. He was a tall muscular young fellow and would have been handsome had it not been for a look of malicious cunning and wickedness in his small dark eyes. But the gift of the mirror pleased his savage fancy greatly and he accepted it with a show of friendliness.

There were eleven Indians in the party. John could not repress a smile when he saw the singed hair and burned face of the young brave whom Ree had knocked into the fire, but even Kingdom failed to recognize the savage with whom he had battled for his very life alone in the darkness. By sign or otherwise neither of the boys made any reference to the adventure of the day and night before, but with perfect friendliness conducted the Indians to their camp.

Tom Fish's spirits had grown lighter when he saw that a fight would be avoided and he greeted each Indian in his happy-go-lucky fashion.

"You're a good un," he said to the chief. "Got a little muscle, too, ain't ye? Ain't no religion in that eye o' your'n, though!"

And so it went with the whole party. As he noticed the buck who was burned Tom laughed aloud. "Pretty near took the hide off, didn't it, Smart Alec?" he exclaimed. "Doubled ye up like a two-bladed jack-knife, I should guess. Oh, these here boys are frisky! No foolin' with them!"

John laughed at this, but no one took heed of him except Tom, who laughed boisterously, as he always did when anyone showed an appreciation of his crude jokes.

Almost immediately upon reaching the camp the Indians asked for "fire-water," but Ree shook his head. It was true that in one of the several packages of goods there was a large stone bottle of whiskey which Capt. Bowen had provided for the boys together with other medicines, but not for a great deal would Kingdom have let the Indians know it; and he hoped that Tom would not find it out, either; for the truth was that Fish had drunk more than was good for him at Pittsburg. But all the savages ate of the meat which was placed before them, and Tom Fish, never neglecting an opportunity of this kind, made out a square meal also. The boys joining in, too, there was quite a feast.

One of the Indians, a good looking young buck, showed for Ree a warmer friendship than any of the others. He was the one whom the boy had mistaken for the chief of the party the day before. His name was Fishing Bird and the chief's name was Big Buffalo. The latter was far from showing entire friendship and a dispute arose between these two savages when Ree told them that he and John wished to purchase land.

Fishing Bird indicated that the boys must go to the great chief of their tribe, Hopocon, or Captain Pipe, as the whites called him, at the village of the Delawares. Big Buffalo, on the other hand, contended that he himself had power to sell land.

Ree rightly judged as he saw an ugly feeling between these two, that he had made a serious mistake when he had mistaken Fishing Bird for the chief the day before, arousing the other's jealousy very much. He thought now, that he recognized in Fishing Bird the Indian with whom he had grappled in the forest. If this were true, it was evident that that Indian, unwilling to confess how he had been vanquished, had said nothing to the others of his struggle with the escaped prisoner.

However, seeing that the land question might cause trouble, both Ree and John dropped it, having learned from the savages that a day's journey to the south and west would take them to the Delawares' town. They determined, therefore, to visit the village of Captain Pipe and talk with the great chief himself.

The afternoon was nearly spent before the Indians departed. They were scarcely gone when Tom Fish called Ree and John to him and the boys noticed for the first time that a great change had come over the old hunter, who for some time had little or nothing to say.

"Did ye see that fresh scalp hangin' at that Buffalo varmint's belt?" he asked. "That means blood. It means fightin'! I've seen many a Redskin, but I never seen a wickeder one than that Buffalo. An' there's no more play for Thomas Trout, which some calls Fish, my kittens, both! I tell ye now, that from what I seed, there was nothin' kept us out of a fight this day but the friendliness o' that chap Fishin' Bird. If Big Buffalo had a' dared, he'd a' pitched onto us. Them's my honest sentiments; an' more'n that, did ye see the scalp at that red devil's belt? Don't tell me they ain't been on the warpath! Did ye see that scalp, an' the blood on it hardly more 'n dry? Oh, sorry day! Oh, sorry day—the blood on it hardly more'n dry. 'Cause I'm a plagued sight mistaken, kittens both, if I don't know whose scalp that is! Oh, sorry day!"

Tom's voice had sunk almost to a whisper and involuntarily John shuddered. The sinking sun cast thick, dark shadows in the narrow valley, and a death-like silence was broken only by the soughing wind and the tinkle of the brook.

These melancholy surroundings and the gruesome way in which Tom spoke, were enough to remove all cheerfulness which might have existed, but Tom said again, slowly and with a mournful emphasis, "I know—I know whose scalp it is, lads; an' the blood on it hardly more'n dry."

The rough woodsman put his arm across his eyes and leaned mournfully on his rifle, as he spoke.

CHAPTER X.

A Night With the Indians.

To shut out from his thoughts the horrid memory of the bloody scalp at Big Buffalo's belt, Ree turned and busied himself with the fire, which had burned quite low, and soon a roaring blaze was leaping skyward, shedding good cheer around.

The woodsman still stood leaning on his rifle, a look of sadness on his face such as was seldom seen there. If John had noticed this he might not have asked in the tone in which he did:

"Well, whose scalp is it?"

"It ain't your'n, kitten, an' ye can be glad o' that."

"Shucks! How can you tell whose it might have been? How could anybody tell?" asked the boy.

Tom made no reply, and Ree deftly changed the subject by saying that one of them had better stand guard that night. He expected no trouble with the Indians, but he was not willing to be caught napping by the unknown foe whose work had now cost the life of their horse.

Tom was gloomy all the evening as they sat before the fire, but he told the boys of the great chief of the Delaware's, Hopocon, or Capt. Pipe, and reminded them that he was one of the Indians who were responsible for the burning of Col. Crawford at the stake eight years earlier.

That and other stories of this noted chief made the boys curious to see him, and anxious to put themselves on friendly terms with him. It was decided that the next day they should visit the Delaware town and make arrangements for securing land. Without a horse they could move their goods only with great labor, and they were desirous of knowing just where they were taking their property, therefore, before they undertook to move it from their present camp.

"Guess I will stay an' watch here, whilst you youngsters go to see Capt. Pipe," said Tom, as the subject was under discussion. "I might not be as peaceful as a little lamb—plague take their greasy skins! Not if I clapped my eyes on that Buffalo critter ag'in!"

"Look a-here, Tom," Ree answered, earnestly. "We boys are on a peaceable mission and we don't want to get into trouble on your account. We know that the horrible sight of that scalp, and your belief that you know from where it came, has made you want revenge, but John and I have had no special trouble with the Delawares and it would be very foolish, situated as we are, for you or any of us to start a fight with them now."

"I see all that—I ain't so blind! But—" Tom did not finish the sentence. Instead he began talking of other things and advised the boys to take every precaution against being treacherously dealt with when they should find Big Buffalo at his own home—the Delaware town.

It was a windy, cloudy morning that found Ree and John tramping through the valleys and over the hills of a fine, thickly wooded country toward the Indian village. Early in the afternoon they came to a sloping hillside beyond which lay a swampy tract grown up to brush and rushes. Close by was a beautiful little lake and at the opposite side the smoke was rising from the town of the Delaware tribe of Indians.

As the boys approached the water, planning to walk around the lake, they were discovered by three Indians in a canoe, which seemed almost to spring out of the water, so quickly did it appear from around a bushy point. The savages headed directly toward the boys, without a sound.

The lads laid down their rifles as a sign of friendliness, and in another minute a swift stroke of a paddle grounded the Indians' craft upon the beach. The Redskins bounded ashore and with some reluctance shook hands with the boys.

Without loss of time Ree gave them to understand that he wished them to inform their chief, Hopocon, or Capt. Pipe, that two young Palefaces were waiting to call on him, and tell of their friendly wish to buy some land of the Delawares, and that they would remain where they were while he should send a canoe to carry them over.

None of the three Indians had been in the party of the previous day, but they seemed readily to comprehend what was desired of them and turned to go.

One of the Redskins, quite a young fellow, lingered behind. After the other two had taken their places in the canoe he pushed it out into deep water, then he made a running jump to leap, aboard. He might have done so very nicely, had he not slipped just as he jumped. As it was, he went sprawling in the water most ridiculously.

The other Indians grunted derisively. John laughed heartily and Ree smiled, amused to see the proud young buck get just such a ducking as he deserved for trying to "show off."

However, the lithe young fellow seized the canoe and was safely in it in a very brief space of time. Soon it was far out on the lake, rocking and dancing lightly as a feather on the fierce little waves, which a strong wind was blowing up.

Ree and John made themselves comfortable on the grassy bank beside the water, and waited. It seemed a long time until they saw a canoe coming for them. The fact was, and the boys shrewdly surmised it, that Capt. Pipe, or Hopocon, desirous of impressing the strangers with his greatness, purposely kept them waiting awhile.

The canoe sent for the boys was manned by two of the Indians they first met, and the lads were taken aboard. Although frail in appearance, the light little craft was capable of carrying seven or eight persons. It was made of the bark of a bitter-nut hickory, and was the first of the kind in which the Connecticut lads had ever ridden. They quickly found that they must aid in keeping the canoe balanced to prevent its upsetting, and their efforts to do this, before they caught the knack of it, rather amused the Indians.

In a short time, however, the canoe touched shore before the Indian town and the Paleface visitors were conducted at once to the council house. This was a long low building, its lower part being built of logs but its sides and roof being of bark. It was open at one end, and at the other end skins were hung up to shut out the wind. In the center of the rude structure, whose floor was only the hard-trodden earth, was a fire, the smoke escaping through a large hole in the roof.

All these things were observed by the boys in time, but first to attract their notice as they entered, were the Indians, especially one of great size—elderly and very dignified, seated on a bear skin spread over a mat of bark. He shook hands with each as they stepped up, saying only "How."

Ree answered in the same fashion but John was so flustrated that he stammered: "How do you do, sir?" in a manner which bored him a great deal, as Ree jokingly recalled the circumstance long afterward.

But Capt. Pipe knew from the lad's tone that he spoke respectfully and it pleased him. Other Indians seemed to feel the same, and the several minor chiefs and medicine men who were present, shook hands with the boys with a great show of dignity and formality. Then the young traders stated the object of their visit and were shown to a seat opposite Capt Pipe and pipes were brought out. They all smoked, the boys soon discovering that it was not tobacco but "kinnikinick"— the inner bark of young willow sprouts dried and pulverized—which was in the pipes.

Presently the great chief laid aside his pipe, a long-stemmed affair with a curiously carved clay bowl, and all others immediately followed his example. In another minute the speech-making began.

Capt. Pipe's was the first address, a brief preliminary statement. He made a most imposing appearance as he stood very erect, his arms folded, his head-dress of feathers reaching half way to the ground behind him, the fringes of his shirt-like coat rustled by the movements of his body, as he talked. Others followed, but the boys understood very little of what was said. As Big Buffalo arose, however, there was a scowl on his face which was far from pleasant. His gestures indicated hostility and the Paleface lads knew that at heart he hated them. They wished Fishing Bird were present to say a friendly word.

Capt. Pipe, himself, spoke a second time a little later, however, and very earnestly Ree and John studied his grave and stern, but not unkind, face, to learn how he felt toward them. They could scarcely believe that he was the savage, who, only a few years before, had been a leading spirit in the torture of Colonel Crawford.

Occasionally the chief used a few English words and the boys gathered from the general trend of his remarks that they would be welcome if they came only as traders; but that settlers were not welcome, and the Indians wished no one to come among them who would clear land or do anything which might lead to the establishing of a settlement of the whites in their country. A reasonable number of hunters and traders might come and go unmolested but there must be no building of permanent cabins; there must be no different life than that led by the children of the forest—the Indians themselves.

A long silence followed this address, and then Ree arose to speak. His heart beat fast, and John trembled inwardly as his friend began. But nervous as he was, there was no weakness in Ree's tones. He spoke slowly and distinctly, using every sign which could be expressed by look or gesture to make his meaning clear; and looking the Indians squarely in the eyes they did not fail to understand as the boy thus told them in his own way, that he and his friends hoped to live at peace with them; that there was but a very small party of them, himself and one other, besides a woodsman who was temporarily with them, and that they had journeyed to that beautiful country of the Delawares to hunt and trade and make themselves a home.

They had not been taught to live as the Indians lived, he said, and they could not have a home without some cleared land about it for the crops which they would need. For this land, Ree went on, they were willing to pay a fair price, and they were desirous of selecting a location that they might get their cabin built. The spot they had chosen was where the course of the river had changed at some time, years before, leaving a little clearing.

As Ree finished speaking he stepped up and laid his presents—two small mirrors and a handsome hunting knife—before Capt. Pipe. John followed his example in this, and there were grunts of approval from all the Indians except Big Buffalo, as the boys sat down.

More speech-making followed, however, taking so much time that John whispered: "If they don't stop soon, or ask us to stay all night, we will have to climb a tree, somewhere."

At last a decision was reached that the boys were to have a piece of land including the clearing to which Ree had referred, and as much of the river valley and adjacent hillsides as they reasonably needed, in exchange for articles to be selected from their stock of goods.

By close attention Ree had been able to understand the matter fairly well, but as the talk of the Indians had seemed so monotonous, John had let his thoughts run to other subjects. He had been wondering what had become of the scalp they had seen at Big Buffalo's belt the day before, and whether Tom Fish really knew the person whose death it signified; and if so, who that person might be. He did not know then, all that he came to know afterward.

With hand-shaking all around the council was concluded, and Capt. Pipe conducted the boys to the feast which the squaws had been preparing. There was broiled venison (without salt) and a sort of soup containing broken corn and beans cooked together in a large kettle.

Nearly all of the Indians who had been in the council partook of these dainties and many others did likewise. Ree and John ate heartily though they did not exactly relish the lack of cleanliness displayed by the savages in their manner of cooking, and in their eating.

The squaws and Indian boys and girls, and many a young brave for that matter, watched the young Palefaces curiously, and their eyes followed the lads closely as Capt. Pipe led them away to his own bark cabin. It was then that John first saw Gentle Maiden, Capt. Pipe's daughter. She was truly handsome for one of her race, but she stepped behind a screen of skins and was gone before Ree had even noticed her.

The chief of the Delawares told the boys to make themselves comfortable, and a squaw, who seemed to be his wife, spread skins for them to sit upon or lie upon, as they chose. Capt. Pipe then gave his guests to understand that they might come and go as they chose and remain with him as long as they wished. He then withdrew and presently the boys did go for a stroll about the queer town of the Indians. Fortunately they met Fishing Bird and he walked all about with them then, leading the way to a fire before which a game like dice was being played.

The seeds of wild plums, colored black on one side and scraped white on the other, were shaken up in a box made of bark and thrown out upon a smooth spot on the ground. The Indians endeavored to throw as many as possible of the seeds with the white sides up, and he who did the best at this, won the game. It seemed very dull amusement to John, but Ree watched the game with much interest, until Fishing Bird beckoned him away. And then something took place which made Ree quite certain that this was the Indian whom he might have killed as they struggled alone in the forest solitude only the second night previous.

It was a wrestling match which Fishing Bird proposed, and he called to a strapping young savage and challenged him to undertake to put Ree down. The brave smiled and stepped up willingly. Ree would have preferred that such a contest had not been suggested, but as the young Indian looked at him in a way which seemed to say, "It will not take me long to put you on your back," he decided to throw the proud young redskin if he could.

With many manifestations of delight the Indians gathered around, as they quickly learned what was taking place; for there was nothing in which the forest rovers had a greater delight than trials of strength and endurance.

Ree stipulated but one thing, as he threw off his coat and made ready, this was that the wrestling should be "catch-as-catch-can."

Ready assent was given, a space was cleared and an Indian clapped his hands as a signal for the contest to begin. Like a panther the young brave sprang toward his sturdy white opponent to catch him "Indian hold." But he reckoned without knowledge of his man. Ree had not forgotten the teachings of Peter Piper, and so cleverly did he dodge, and so quickly seize the Indian about the legs, that in a twinkling the proud buck was stretched upon the earth.

There were expressions of wonderment from the Indians, but in a second the vanquished redskin was on his feet, anxious for another trial.

John, with utter disregard of good manners, was laughing heartily over his friend's success, and as Ree declined to wrestle any more, the Indian turned to him, and somewhat fiercely demanded that he should try conclusions with him.

John glanced at Ree and the latter nodded for him to go ahead. In another minute then, a match, the closeness and desperation of which delighted the savages beyond measure, was in progress.

Tightly clasping each other's arms, the contestants strained every muscle and struggled back and forth and round and round—now slowly, now with movements most rapid, neither gaining an advantage. Longer and longer the contest continued in this way, and Ree saw that John was becoming worn out. He must act quickly or succumb to the Indian's greater weight and power of endurance.

"You can throw him if you only say to yourself that you must and that you will, and then do it," Ree whispered, as John was pushed near him, and his advice was taken.

With a show of strength which surprised them all, John forced his opponent backward, and tried again to trip the fellow, but could not. Then he allowed the savage to try to trip him, and seizing the opportunity, gave the redskin so sudden and violent a pull that he was taken off his feet and fell heavily, dragging John down with him. Both the Indian's shoulders touched the ground, however, and with savage glee the redskins acknowledged John to be the victor. To do them justice, they seemed not at all put out that their man was defeated. Only one who was present scowled. He was Big Buffalo, and with an ugly look he strode away from the campfire's light.

Ree could not help but notice the savage fellow's hostile manner. "We better watch out for him," he said to John as they discussed the incident sometime later, when they had sought rest for the night on the skins in Capt. Pipe's house.

"It makes me feel—well, not exactly comfortable, Ree," John answered. "Here we are a hundred miles from civilization sleeping in the hut of one of the bloodiest Indians of the Northwest Territory; Indians all around us, and Goodness knows what else in the woods, on every side!"

"Why, John," said Ree, "I believe we are safer to-night than at any time since we left Fort Pitt. Capt. Pipe may be a bad Indian, but he would fight for us, if need be, while we are his guests. He might scalp us to-morrow after we have said goodbye, but when we are in his house as friends, we will be protected."

CHAPTER XI.

Again a Hidden Enemy.

The boys were early astir the following morning. As soon as they were up Capt. Pipe's wife placed a dish of boiled corn, like hominy, before them, and this was their breakfast. A little later, telling Capt. Pipe of the great amount of work they had to do, the lads bade him good-bye, the chief giving them each a pouch of parched corn, and sending an Indian to take them in a canoe across the lake.

It was two hours past noon when Tom Fish suddenly started up from the broiled turkey with which he was regaling himself, as he heard some one approach, and discovered Ree and John returning. He greeted them gladly, but not in his usual hilarious fashion, and they could not but notice how unlike himself he was as he carved for them some juicy slices from the fine young gobbler he had cooked. Yet he listened with interest to Ree's account of their trip, John often breaking in with such jolly comment as: "You should have heard those Indians talk! Why they beat a quilting bee for gabbling, except that they didn't all talk at once."

"But they are real orators," added Ree quite soberly. "I've heard that an Indian has three ambitions—to be a mighty hunter, a great warrior and a grand orator; and there are some splendid speakers among the Delawares."

"The's some red-handed, bloody murderers among 'em, too, I kin tell ye," Tom Fish growled. "I got no rest whilst ye was gone, a thinkin' of it."

"Has anything happened, Tom?" asked Ree, struck by his friends grave manner.

"Cheer up, Thomas, cheer up!" cried John. "You've been about as cheerful company as a box of indigo ever since you saw that—that hideous thing at Big Buffalo's belt."

"Well, it's a wonder the' didn't nothing happen, an' somethin's goin' to happen, I know," the hunter replied to Ree's question, ignoring John's bantering, as he often did. "That Buffalo varmint means harm. I've been thinkin' it all over an' the' ain't no two ways about it. If I ain't a sight mistaken, I seen him peekin' down from the hill back there, not a half hour ago—either him or some dirty Mingo; I didn't exactly see him, but I heard some one, an' I'd a' peppered away at him if you kittens hadn' 'a been gone an' me not knowin' just where ye might be. So I've been thinkin' it all over, an' mighty sorry I am I ever piloted ye into this hostyle kentry. The's only one thing to do, an' that's to take what stuff ye kin an' get back to Pittsburg fast as yer legs kin take ye. Now as fer me, I kin take care of myself, but I'll see ye part way anyhow, an' I'd go clear back with ye if I didn't have somethin' very important to 'tend to."

Ree could not help but smile at Tom's drooping spirits, though the discouraging talk made it necessary for him to appear really more cheerful than he felt, as he realized that Big Buffalo really seemed anxious to cause trouble. But he shook his head at John, as he saw the latter about to scold Tom for bringing them into this part of the wilderness only to advise them to leave it; for his chum's face showed that he was not pleased with Tom's manner.

"There is just one thing to be done," Ree exclaimed.

"An' that's get right back—" Tom Fish was saying.

But the youthful leader of the party interrupted: "Go back? No, sir! The one thing to do is to go forward, and take our goods with us without further loss of time. We will get a good, stout cabin up and then we'll be better prepared for trouble if it comes. And that prowler, you heard, Tom, must have been the same cowardly wretch who shot old Jerry. We must watch for him. We cannot be too careful, but if he is the same fellow who fired on us and nearly killed Black Eagle's son, 'way back on the Pennsylvania border, I think I can guess who it is, and I can tell you, he is a coward. But let's get to work."

"I like yer spunk, lad, an' I like you, but what I want to say is, that Tom Trout as some calls Fish, will stick by ye till ye get some sort of a shack throwed up, anyhow."

"Bully for you, Tom! And bully for you, too, Ree," exclaimed John springing up to begin whatever task awaited him. "I was beginning to get away down in the mouth, the way Tom was talking a minute ago."

"We must take the goods out of the cart and pack them in convenient shape for carrying," Ree directed, without further ado. "By dragging a few things forward a hundred rods or so, then coming back for more and so on, we should reach the river in a couple of days."

And so all fell to work with a will. The cart did not contain a heavy load, as it would have been impossible for old Jerry to have hauled it through the woods, up hills, across streams and boggy places. But when it came to carrying forward everything except the cart, which must be abandoned, without the aid of a horse, the task was found to be a most laborious one.

The unpacking and rearranging consumed so much time that darkness had come on before the last bundle of the merchandise and provisions had been carried forward to the first stopping place, a little way beyond the top of the bluff, in the valley below which the camp had been.

While John and Tom erected a shelter for the night, for the wind was cold and raw, Ree returned to the valley to procure coals with which to start a fire at the new camp. He found it necessary to enliven the dying embers with a few fresh sticks of wood, and as he stooped over to blow greater life into the struggling blaze which started up, he heard a rustling in the leaves on the hill behind him, in the direction opposite that in which his friends were. Like a flash he sprang away from the fire into the half-darkness which filled the valley. He was in the nick of time. A rifle cracked and a bullet threw up the ashes and sent the sparks flying where his head had been just a second before.

With the speed of the wind Ree ran in the direction from which the shot had come, his own rifle cocked and ready. He thought he heard some one making off in the darkness as he reached the top of the hill, but whether white man or Indian—Delaware or Mingo, he could not tell. He called out a command to halt, but no attention was given his order for the uncertain sound of fleeing footsteps continued. He chanced a shot in the direction of the unknown enemy, although he realized it would probably do no good.

While he reloaded his rifle Ree stepped behind a tree, and a few seconds later John came running up. As it was too dark to continue the chase, both boys returned to camp, stopping in the ravine to secure a fire brand to start a blaze to prepare their supper. In vain did John ask questions as to whom Ree believed the would-be murderer was; they could not be answered, for, as Ree said, he had not seen the person.

Tom Fish, disconsolate as he well could be, sat on a big bundle of merchandise as the boys rejoined him.

"It's sure death to stay here, lads," were the first words he said, and his tone was not calculated to make the young travelers comfortable; but resolving to look on the brighter side, Ree cheerily answered:

"A man is in some danger wherever he is. We will all feel better when we smell some venison on the hot coals. And just wait till we get our cabin built! We are going to get some beans and late squashes from the Indians, and bake some corn bread, and have a regular old-fashioned Connecticut supper!"

"Did ye hit him, d'ye think, Ree?" asked Tom, brightening up.

"No, but he scared him into eleven kinds of fits," John answered for his friend, catching the spirit of the latter's courage and enthusiasm.

"It ain't that I am caring for myself. Tom Fish, or Tom Trout didn't ever lose a wink o' sleep bein' afraid he couldn't look out for number one," the woodsman went on. "But after—after that—thing we saw the other day—but I guess we've got our appetites left," he said, suddenly changing the subject.

It was not long until the supper was ready and eaten and all did feel much the better for it, as Ree had predicted. The ordinary noises of the forest, the howling of wolves, in pursuit of some poor deer, perhaps, the far-away shriek of a panther balked of its prey, it may have been, gave them little concern. Though the darkness was intense and enemies might draw very near without being observed, the boys believed they had made peace with the Indians and the presence of four-footed enemies did not worry them.

Tom Fish felt very differently about the matter of the Indians' friendship, but he kept these thoughts to himself for the time being, and though there are far more comfortable places than a camp in a great wilderness on a cold November night, the lads from Connecticut would have been entirely happy had it not been for the mystery of the strange prowler, the thought that several times they had been secretly fired upon, and that there was no knowing when another attack might be made in which the aim of the dastardly assailant need be but a trifle better to end the life of one or both of them, perhaps.

Yet, even these gloomy facts could not dispel the good spirits which accompany good health and the hopefulness of youth. Even Tom seemed to forget his dark forebodings as he was persuaded to tell a number of stories of his own adventures. Quite comfortable, therefore, though on the alert to catch the first sound of danger's coming, the little party sat for an hour or two beneath the rude shelter which had been erected, while the firelight performed its fantastic feats around them.

Tom volunteered to remain on guard the first part of the night, and crept out at the back of their little house of poles and brush, that he might not be observed, should anyone be watching. Then, softly through the darkness he made his way to a convenient tree against which he leaned, in the dark shadows. Ree and John, wrapped in their blankets on their beds of deerskins spread over the autumn leaves, were soon asleep.

A heavy snow was sifting through the swaying branches of the trees when Tom called Ree and the latter went on watch. This change in the weather gave the quick-witted sentinel an idea. With the first streak of dawn he called John to prepare breakfast, then hurried back to the valley where their cart had been left, taking care to observe that there were no tracks of any human creature along the way. From the box of the abandoned two-wheeled wagon he secured two good sized boards and carried them to camp.

John watched in open-mouthed astonishment as he saw Ree coming up with the lumber, but in a minute or two he discovered what his friend designed to do. With no other tools than an axe and auger he soon built a sled large and strong enough to carry all their goods.

Ree's idea proved an excellent one. The snow-fall was just enough to make a sled run smoothly, and by a little after sunrise "all the property of Kingdom and Jerome, Indian traders and home-seekers," as John expressed it, was piled upon the pair of runners which the senior member of the firm had contrived, and they and Tom Fish were steadily drawing it toward their long-sought destination.

"We must reach the Cuyahoga river by night," Ree urged, and his own determination gave strength to himself and his companions. Up hill and down hill they hurried, tugging, perspiring, making the best speed possible through the silent forest.

And as the sun burst through a sea of gray-black clouds, and shone brilliantly just before night's coming, it seemed an omen of good to the little party in the wilderness, for at almost the same moment, Ree, running on a head a little way, cried: "Here we are!"

Before the daylight closed, the site of the cabin, work on which was to begin the next day, had been selected on the long irregular mound close to the river, which has already been described.

Ree called attention to the natural advantages of the place—its sides sloping down in three directions while on the fourth side and thirty feet below was the river. It was a point which could be defended in case of an attack, and the additional fact of the natural clearing and fertile lands surrounding it, made the place seem most desirable.

"The's only one thing the matter with this location," said Tom Fish, surveying the mound from the semi-circular valley around it, as the twilight settled down. "The's likely to be ague in a place like this, it bein' so nigh the water. It's a mighty good thing to steer clear of, ague is."

"But there are so many natural advantages," Ree persisted, "and our cabin will be well up in the air and the sunlight."

"That's a good point, Ree," John put in, "but think of it—we will have to carry all our firewood up that hill."

"I'll carry the wood if you play out, old chap," was the answer and the matter ended by Ree having his own way, as was generally the case, not because he was selfish or obstinate, but because he was sure he was right before he made up his mind, and because he had that born spirit of leadership which gave himself and all others confidence in his decisions and actions.

Although careful observation during the day had failed to reveal any sign of their prowling foe, whoever he might be, Ree and John agreed to divide the guard duty of the night between them. Ree took the first watch and reported all quiet when John relieved him at midnight.

When daylight came John went a little way up the wooded hillside opposite the mound to pick up some dry wood for their fire. Suddenly he stopped and a startled look came upon his face. There in the snow were foot-prints made by moccasined feet. They followed the trail the sled had made the day before, up to the very edge of the clearing in which their camp was made.

There, John found, as he guardedly investigated, they circled off to one side a little way, hovered about, here and there, then re-crossed the sled's track and disappeared in the woods. What could it mean? Instantly he remembered that the foot-prints of the person who had several times fired upon their camp, had been made by boots. He hurried to the camp mentally ejaculating: "What will Tom Fish say of this?"

Tom was still asleep, but Ree had commenced the breakfast. "It is too bad," he said, thinking aloud, as he learned of John's discovery. "I suppose we ought to follow those tracks if only for safety's sake, and find out who made them, but I do hate to lose the time when we ought to be getting a cabin built."

The discovery was pointed out to Tom when he awoke a little later.

"A prowlin' Mingo!" the old hunter exclaimed as he inspected the foot-prints. "Kittens both, the's trouble brewin'. It's a wonder the varmint didn't shoot. I don't see what he's up to, always doggin' us this way! But I'll tell ye what I'll do. You lads get yer axes an' go to work, an' I'll foller up them tracks. An' bust my galluses, kittens both, I'll give the varmint a dose as'll make him think of his pore ol' granddad, if I ketch him!"

Tom's suggestion found favor at once, though the boys could not explain the varying moods of their friend, which made him cool and courageous one day and dejected and fearful another. But breakfast being over, Tom set out.

"Be careful," Ree called after him. "Don't get yourself or us into any row with the Delawares, unnecessarily." The hunter made no answer.

CHAPTER XII.

Building a Cabin.

By reason of having been the first to see the strange foot-prints, and having come upon them, too, in the gray light of the early morning, when alone in the forest solitudes, John found it hard to shake off the dread with which they filled him. On the other hand, Ree was bright and chipper as a squirrel in the nutting season. He reasoned that the discovery of the tracks was fortunate, rather than otherwise, for it proved that their mysterious enemy was still hovering on their trail and gave them an opportunity of finding out who the wretch might be. And they now knew that they must be constantly on their guard, while except for the discovery, they might have become careless and fallen easy victims to their sneaking foe.

So he cheered John up, and loud and clear the sounds of their axes rang out in the crisp, delightful air of the woods. Both boys threw off their coats as the healthful perspiration came to their faces and hands, and their vigor and strength seemed to grow rather than decrease as they worked. They had been careful to keep their axes sharp, and the chips flew almost in showers.

The trees selected for cutting were those from five to eight inches in diameter, whose trunks were firm and straight. The lads would be able to handle logs of this size, while larger ones would give them trouble, especially as they no longer had a horse to draw them to the cabin site. The work would be hard at best, but no more than the boys had expected, and the hearty good will with which they set about the task before them, promised its speedy accomplishment in spite of obstacles.

For mutual safety the boys remained near one another as they worked, and timber was so plentiful that their progress was not interfered with by this arrangement. Their rifles were within reach, and their eyes and ears were alert.

The hour of noon brought a brief but pleasant rest, and the afternoon slipped quickly away. As supper time drew near, John, having had only a cold lunch at noon, was becoming very hungry and was about to mention that fact, when, instead, he suddenly seized his rifle and sprang behind a tree. At the same instant Ree did likewise.

"As sure as shooting I heard some one cough!" exclaimed John in an undertone.

"I heard a footstep," Ree quietly answered.

"Ho ho!" It was Tom Fish who called, and coming forward, he confessed that he had been trying the boys' watchfulness by trying to steal up to them without being discovered. He was decidedly surprised to find them so quick to detect his approach, for he had scarcely come within gun shot.

Tom declared to John, however, that he had not coughed, saying it must have been John's alert instinct which told him that some one was drawing near, and made him imagine he heard such a sound. The boys did not agree with him, however, for he also undertook to say that Ree had not heard a footstep at all, but being keenly alive to detect the approach of anyone, had imagined he heard a noise before he really did, all through that peculiar sense which he called instinct.

"But anyway it's a good thing for you, Tom Fish, that you hollered when you did," said John. "I was just on the point of giving you a dose of these lead pills that you are so everlastingly talking about!"

Tom's face lengthened. "You don't want to be too quick with your pill box, boy," said he. "You want to see what an' who you're shootin' at. Great Snakes, now! What if ye had peppered away at me?"

"Well, don't come creeping up like a sneaking Mingo then," laughed John, and Ree, who knew that John had not seen Tom until after he called, and had been really frightened, joined in his chum's merriment.

"But tell us what you found, Tom," urged Ree.

"Well, I'll tell ye," Tom slowly and very soberly answered, "I don't know what to make of it. Them tracks was made by a redskin an' they came straight to the camp along the trail we made yesterday. Then after leaving here, they strike off an' go straight to the little lake across from the Delaware town, an' there they stop. It's plain as kin be, that some varmint from that there town has been spyin' on us. Now was it the same critter as killed the horse, or wa'n't it? An' if it was, was that critter the Buffalo chap? An' what was he hangin' 'round here ag'in for last night?"

These questions furnished an abundance of material for conversation during the evening meal, but no definite answers were agreed upon. Ree would not admit that they were in danger from the Delawares, though he agreed that Big Buffalo was a bad Indian. He was quite sure, however, that Big Buffalo had not shot old Jerry, for the Indian was at the head of the party of savages he had encountered the morning after the horse was shot, and had plainly been surprised to see any white person so far west.

But these arguments did not satisfy Tom Fish, nor was John at all sure that Ree was right.

After supper Tom said he must go back for a deer which he had killed in the morning, a couple of miles from camp, and which he had hung up beyond the reach of the wolves, until his return. But he had made a short cut in coming back to camp and so had not secured the venison.

John jokingly cautioned him to let them know when he approached the camp in returning, lest he be mistaken for the prowler, and Tom most soberly promised he would, and was at great pains to do so; for he was always at a loss to understand the younger of the two friends, and could not be sure whether he was in sober earnest or only joking, no matter what was said.

The night passed without incident. Tom did more than his share of guard duty, but it became apparent next day that he did not like to wield an axe. He said he would go out for some fresh "provender" and "sort o' earn his keep" that way.

So while Fish went hunting, the boys toiled away. They could not complain because Tom helped so little with the cabin, for they had no right to expect it of him; they were thankful indeed, to have him keep the larder well supplied and to let him sleep during the day, for he took the part of sentinel a large part of every night. This gave the boys opportunity to secure a good rest and to rise each morning eager to continue the task of building.

Their faithful efforts were rapidly being rewarded and in due time the logs for the cabin were all ready. These were chopped into lengths with a view to making their dwelling 12 by 14 feet—no longer than the average bedroom of modern houses, but affording all the space necessary, and being the easier to keep warm by reason of being compact.

No time was spent on "fancy work," as John called it, at that time. A floor and other improvements could be added later. For the main thing to be accomplished was to get a secure shelter ready as soon as possible.

The Indian summer was long since gone, and though there were still warm, pleasant days now and then, cold rains and snow came frequently. No matter what the weather, however, the work went on, though hands and faces were cut and scratched by the brush and chapped by the raw winds.

"Ree, you are a perfect fright," said John with a laugh, one day. "If people from home were to see you now, they would say you would be lucky to find a scarecrow which would trade places with you. And your hair—why, it almost reaches your shoulders!"

Ree smiled but did not at once reply. Then, looking up, he said: "Old boy, we are going back to Connecticut some day, but the time is a long way off. If we go with whole skins and with money in our pockets, it will be an easy matter to get into good clothes and to get our hair cut. What you want to do, is to watch out that some Indian barber does not cut that long hair of yours, rather closer than you like."

It was so seldom that Ree joked, and he spoke now in so droll a way, that Tom Fish laughed boisterously. It had been long since the boys had heard him so merry; for, though he never mentioned that subject, the remembrance of the scalp Big Buffalo had carried, seemed always on his spirits, bearing him down to a melancholy, unnatural mood.

They did not understand it then; they did not know.

When the time came to raise the cabin—that is, to fit the logs in place one upon another, after they had been dragged and rolled to the summit of the mound, to be in readiness, Tom's help was found most valuable, and both Ree and John appreciated his work. But notwithstanding, they would have been better pleased had he not remained with them. He had shown so much ill-feeling toward the Indians who had come about from time to time, that there was reason to believe he would commit some rash act which would make trouble for all.

They could not tell Tom they did not trust him. They could not tell him to go. Ree's repeated cautions that they must avoid getting into difficulty with the redskins, were the only hints that could be given.

Capt. Pipe himself and a large number of his braves visited the camp when the cabin was nearly finished, to make the settlement for the land the boys had engaged to buy. The young pioneers had twice sent word to him by Indians who were passing, that they wished to make their payment and enter into a final agreement, and he had at last sent messengers to say that he would visit them on a certain day. On the day before Capt. Pipe's expected visit Ree and John went hunting to secure an abundance of meat for a feast for their guests. It was the first day they had spent away from the hard work on their cabin, except for Sundays when they bathed and gave their clothes needed attention, and no two boys ever enjoyed a holiday more. There was some snow—not enough to make walking difficult, but really an advantage to the young hunters, for it showed them the numerous tracks of the game they sought.

To this day, men, who have heard the stories handed down from generation to generation, of the hunters' paradise in what is now the Northern part of Ohio, in the years before 1800, delight to tell of the abundance of choicest game found in the valley of the Cuyahoga and about the small lakes in its vicinity, and Ree and John were in that very locality years before the white man's axe had opened up the country to general settlement, driving the deer, the bear and wolves and all kindred animals away.

Little wonder is it that these hardy pioneer boys were constantly reminding themselves that they must pass by many fine opportunities for a good shot, because of the necessity of saving their powder and bullets for actual use; there must be no shooting except when there was a good chance of securing game of some value.

Little wonder is it, that, even under these circumstances, Ree, by the middle of the afternoon, had secured a deer and three turkeys besides a big rabbit which he caught in his hands as it sprang from its burrow beneath a fallen tree-top. And John had also shot a deer and had killed their first bear—a half-grown cub which, late in finding quarters for its long winter's sleep, rose on its hind legs, growling savagely, as the boys came suddenly upon it, in passing around a great boulder in the river valley.

In good time on a certain Tuesday in December, Capt. Pipe and his party arrived. Some of the braves were inclined to be very frolicsome and it was necessary to watch that they did not get their hands on property which was not their own.

But their chief was all dignity. He seemed to take a fancy to Ree, who was scarcely less dignified than himself,—being so grave and quiet in his deportment, indeed, that a doughty warrior who had made up his mind to challenge him to wrestle, had not the courage to suggest the contest.

The business of the day sat lightly on John's mind, however, and he was full of antics as any of the redskins. It resulted in his being challenged to wrestle, and he was laid on his back in short order. Then he remembered Ree's advice at the time he wrestled at the Delaware town, and making use of it, threw his man after a most clever and spirited contest.

But the great feature of the day, in John's estimation, was the foot race in which he defeated a young Indian known to be one of the best runners of the tribe, winning a beautiful pair of leggings which Big Buffalo put up in a wager. It was a short-distance race and he realized that in a longer run the Indian would have defeated him; it made him decide to practice running long distances. He might wish to outrun the redskins to save his scalp, some day.

Tom Fish sat silent and alone, a little apart from all the others, during the whole time. He eyed Big Buffalo sharply when no one save Ree observed him, but the gruesome scalp no longer hung at the Indian's belt.

Fishing Bird was there and seemed especially friendly, though, not being a sub-chief, as was Big Buffalo, he did not pretend to any special dignity, but enjoyed himself in sports with the other young Indians and John.

When at last the Delawares settled down to business, there was a great deal of talk before an agreement was reached, that the boys should have a tract embracing about 200 acres, which the Indians marked off, in exchange for three red blankets and a bolt of blue cloth. It was a rather dear price, John thought, but Ree declared it was a bargain, for they secured just the land they wanted. Moreover, they retained the friendship of the Indians, and even though they should be obliged to pay for the land a second time to the United States government or the State of Connecticut, they could well afford to do so, under these circumstances.

There was general hand-shaking as the Delawares went away, though Tom Fish discreetly disappeared for the time, vowing he would give his hand to "no bloody varmint."

The Indians insisted that the young "Long Knives" (Ree and John) should return their visit the second day following, for a ratification of the bargain they had made. This the boys regretted, as it would probably delay the completion of their cabin; but they were obliged to accept the invitation, and did so.

The next day, Wednesday, however, work on their rude dwelling was resumed, and Tom Fish turned in and helped like a good fellow. A fire-place and chimney had already been built of flat stones from along the margin of the river, and this day, so industriously did all apply themselves, that the roof and door were finished and the cabin practically completed except for the improvements to be added from time to time.

Words can hardly express the boys' pleasure as they built a fire for the first time in the big fire-place and found that their chimney did its work admirably. Without loss of time they at once moved into their new house from the brush shack in which their home had been; and by the cheerful fire light, as the night came on, they placed their things in as orderly a manner as possible, and found themselves quite comfortable, though much remained to be done, the chinking of the walls being the chief task unfinished.

Notwithstanding how the wind crept in at the open cracks until this work should be done, the boys were happy as they cooked and ate their supper in their new home. The ripple and murmur of the river as it splashed on the shore or washed over half-hidden stones, rose to them from the foot of the mound, and was like sweet music in their ears. The wind gently tossed the branches of the trees in harmony with the water's sound, and the howling of wolves far off somewhere in the darkness, made the feeling of security which the stout cabin walls gave all the more pleasing. Their prowling foe had not been about since the first night of their arrival, and they felt entirely safe.

"I guess I'll turn in, then," said John, after trying in vain to brighten up Tom Fish and get him to telling stories; and he was soon asleep on the bed of leaves he had made in a corner.

Ree, having had no chance to read since leaving home, resolved to improve this opportunity. He got his "Pilgrim's Progress" from a chest, and settled himself before the fire.

All the evening Tom had sat in silence beside the big chimney, but soon he leaned over, and placing one big hand on Ree's knee, said in a low voice:

"I've been wantin' to tell ye somethin', Ree; it's about that thar scalp that has upset me so ever since I seen it."

CHAPTER XIII.

The Strange Story of Arthur Bridges.

Putting down his book, Ree looked thoughtfully into Tom's face.

"Of course," said he, "John and I have wondered about that—that matter—but we have considered that you had some reason for not talking of it, or telling us what it meant; and it was really none of our business. But I want to say, Tom, that I would rather you would not tell me anything which I must keep from John. He and I—well, you know how we have always been together, and we have no secrets from each other."

"Bless ye, Ree, lad," exclaimed the old woodsman, "ye kin tell him all ye please of what I'm goin' to tell ye. The only reason I don't talk before him is—he's so full o' fun ye know; and ain't always keerful what he says. I don't keer when we're spinnin' yarns; but this here—it ain't no triflin' thing."

"It's John's way. He would not hurt your feelings for anything, Tom."

The hunter did not answer at once, but buried his face in his hands. Ree could plainly see that some great trouble was on his mind. Presently, however, he raised his head, and with a sigh clasped his hands over his knee.

"Arthur Bridges," he began, "was as fine a young feller as ever the Colonies produced; an' excep' for bein' a little wild, ye wouldn't a' asked to clap yer eyes on a promisin'er chap. It was odd he made up t' me the way he did, me bein' old enough to be his father, a'most, but ye see we was both at Valley Forge together, an' all men was brothers there. We had jist one pair o' shoes betwist us,—Art an' me—an' he wore 'em one day, an' me the next, an' so on. When grub was scant, we shared each with t'other, an' when he got down sick I took keer on him.

"Art tol' me all about himself then, an' it was pitiful. His ol' pap back in Connecticut was as pesky an' ol' Tory as ever did the Continental troops a bad turn; but his mother was loyal as anybody could be. She was born an' bred in this kentry, an' her husband had come from England; that was just the difference betwixt 'em, to start on. The upshot on it was, that Art believed as his mother did, an' it was nat'ral as could be that he should run off an' join General Washington's army. That is what he did anyhow, an' his father swore that he hoped the lad would be killed, though his mother was prayin' for his safety night an' day.

"Once in a long time Art would get some word from home—always from his mother, tellin' him to stick true through thick an' thin an' all would come right by an' by. I guess maybe he believed it would, too; but I didn't ever have much hope on it myself. Bein' a little wild, as ye might say, Art got wilder yet in the army, though there was always a great love for his mother in him. But he got so toward the last that he hated his father—yes, hated him fearful. Then for a long stretch he didn't hear nothin' from home an' didn't see anybody as had heard anything about his folks.

"That's how matters stood when the war was over. He says to me as how he was goin' home, anyhow, an' I tol' him he better do that same. As for me, I was always for rovin' an' I lit out for Kaintucky which we was hearin' was a great place for fightin' an' huntin'. So that's how it come about that Art an' me parted company.

"I was in Kaintucky an' 'round thar for more'n four years; some o' the time with Col. Boone an' some o' the time with other chaps. Then I got to longin' to go back east an' I went. I wasn't thinkin' o' meetin' up with Art Bridges again, as I reckoned on him bein' up in Connecticut all settled down an' married, prob'ly. But who should I meet up with one day but Art himself, lookin' wilder an' more reckless than when I seen him last. He comes up to me and slaps me on the shoulder an' calls me by name a'most before I knowed him. An' it did give me a big surprise to see how he had changed; not so much in looks as in his ways. He was that rough like. After a while he tol' me all about himself, an' I could a jist cried tears for him like a baby.

"He had got started home, he tol' me, after the fightin' was over, an' I don't know but he might a' been pretty near there—I don't just remember—but anyhow, who should he meet up with one day in a tavern, but a cousin o' his who looked so much like him they would 'a passed for twins anywhere. This here cousin's name was Ichabod Nesbit, an' the first thing he did when he saw Art was to shake hands with him like they was at a funeral an' say as how he had some awful bad news to tell him. An' then he went on to tell him as how his mother had died months before, an' his ol' pap was livin' on an' cursin' the Colonies with pretty nigh every breath—an' cursin' his own son. This Nesbit feller told Art, too, as how the ol' man had run through all his property an' was livin' alone an' actin' like a crazy man.

"Waal, Art was for goin' back to see the ol' man anyhow, to see if he couldn't do somethin' to straighten him up some; but this cousin, Ichabod, tol' him as how he hadn't better do it, sayin' as how if he could come home an' bring a fortune, folks would say it was all right; but if he was comin' home with only the clothes on his back, why, he had better stay away; because he couldn't do nothin' with his father anyhow. An' somehow this is jist the way Art was brought to look at it, an' it upset him terrible. For of course the soldiers didn't have no pocket full o' money an' it was pretty true, likewise, as how he didn't have much more'n the clothes on his back, jist as Ichabod said. Pretty blue, an' a' most sick from all his plans o' goin' home bein' spoiled, Art turned back right thar and led a rovin' life for years. He was quick an' sharp, an' picked up a livin', but that was 'bout all for he couldn't settle down no place.

"All this an' a lot more 'bout what he had been doin', Art tol' me there in Philadelphia, an' I was for gettin' him to go back west with me. But no, he wouldn't; an' me bein' no hand to make out around the towns, I jist went back to the frontier an' beyond. I was in Kaintucky an' in this northwest kentry clean to Detroit. I got to know Simon Kenton, the Injun fighter, an' I made some big huntin' an' fightin' trips with him an' other fellers.

"An' so time run along till this last summer a year ago, I takes it into my head one day to go east agin; an' when I had my mind made up there was no stoppin' me. I didn't go to Philadelphia right off, but to New York. I wanted to see the big piles o' furs that come in thar.

"Now it turned out that one day in New York who should I meet up with but Joel Downs who was with us—Art an' me—in the army. We was talkin' away thar, when he asked me did I know what had ever become o' Art Bridges? An' it turned out that he went on to tell me then all 'bout how Art's father was dead, an' his mother left alone, workin' hard to manage the farm, though they was well off, because she wanted Art to have a nice place when he come home. For she wouldn't believe the stories that was told around (by Ichabod Nesbit, I've been thinkin') that Art was dead. So she was waitin' an' waitin' for Art to come an' never knowin' how the poor boy had been lied to by his 'ornery cousin, an' thinkin' he'd come some day.

"Waal, ye kin jist guess how I felt when I heard all this! For I saw through it quicker'n wink that that 'ornery Ichabod was tryin' to make folks think Art was dead, an' schemin' to get hold of the property that would be Art's if he ever come home alive. But I never says a word 'bout this to Joel Downs. Not much! I wasn't goin' to have him goin' back to Connecticut tellin' folks as how Art was leadin' a wild life an' goin' to the dogs.

"No, sir; I jist begun huntin' for Art Bridges. I went to Philadelphia first, an' got some track on him, findin' out as how he had gone off to Kaintucky—lookin' for me, I guess. I went off to Kaintucky too, jist as fast as I could. I got some track on him again, as how he had gone back to Philadelphia, We must 'a passed on the road somewheres. Back to Philadelphia I went again, an' found out as how Art had gone west to Duquesne—Fort Pitt, or Pittsburgh they call it now. So I started for Fort Pitt, an' on the way I met up with you young kittens on your way into this red devils' own kentry.

"An' I come on into this kentry because I found out at Fort Pitt that Art had gone on west intendin' to make his way to Detroit, huntin' an' trappin' an' tradin'. He expected to go on to Detroit next spring an' get a place with a big fur company in charge o' some tradin' post or other, away off somewheres, he didn't keer where—he was jist that sick of the kind o' life he was leadin', an' wanted to get 'way off from everybody.

"But that ain't all! There was a man thar as said Ichabod Nesbit had been seen 'round thar, an' he was lookin' for Art Bridges, too. An' I know that that 'ornery cousin was lookin' for Art to murder him. I felt it in my bones. He wanted to be sure Art was dead an' then he would go back an 'pass himself off as Art Bridges an' have the property anyhow. Then when I heard as how Ichabod had passed himself off as Art in one place, I was sure I was right. But he didn't need to do no murder 'nless it was him as hired the bloody varmints to do it for him," and the hunter's voice grew husky, "for that—that thar scalp—it was Art Bridges'—an' oh, if I had been jist a day sooner! For the blood on it was hardly more'n dry!"

Tom Fish sunk his face in his hands and a convulsive half-sob, half-sigh shook his body from head to foot, as though with ague.

Ree Kingdom drew nearer the sorrow-stricken man and took his big hand in his own.

"Tom," he said, "it is a sad, sad story. I know just what you suffer. But listen, Tom. It is not absolutely certain that the scalp we saw was that of your friend. No man could positively swear to it, just by seeing the color of the hair. And here is another thing I have been wanting to tell you, Tom, but I did not like to interrupt you. I know how Arthur Bridges' mother has been waiting and waiting for him to come. I have heard what she has suffered, for she is a sister of a Mrs. Catesby at whose home I lived and who was like a mother to me. But Mrs. Catesby's husband, who is now dead, was not an agreeable man and the sisters hardly ever saw each other. They lived far apart, but now Mrs. Catesby has moved to town and they will be nearer one another. Mrs. Catesby was so kind to me, Tom, that I would be mean indeed if I would not try to help you find her nephew. But I will help you, and if he is now in this part of the country we will hear of him sooner or later through the Indians."

"No, there is only one thing to do, an' it is for me to do it," Tom Fish replied without looking up. "You can't help, Ree, an' ye'd only get into a row an' spoil all yer own plans. It is fer me to squar' accounts—an' I'll—do it. For I tell, ye, Ree, I ain't mistaken. I'd know that silky dark ha'r of Art Bridges' if I seen it in Jerusalem. Oh, it's too bad—it's too bad!"

Ree could make no answer, and in another minute Tom Fish straightened up and said he would turn in. He told Ree to do the same, and as he lay himself down the boy heard him saying:

"We must all die—all die—an' them that's left can only squar' accounts."

Never before had the land of friends and civilization seemed to Ree to be so far away as it did that night. His busy thoughts kept him awake until nearly morning. He knew what Tom Fish meant when he said he would "squar' accounts." In other words he would make the Delawares pay for Art Bridges' death. There would undoubtedly he trouble which would put an end to their plans for trading and home-making in this new country. They could not fight the redskins one day, and be received as peaceable traders the next.

And on the other hand, if Arthur Bridges, a peaceable trader, had been murdered, might he and John not be in greatest danger of the same fate? Was it not true that the Indians were treacherous and not to be trusted though they seemed friendly? Even if Tom began the fight alone, would not the Indians blame him and John as being friends of his, and attack them?

At last Ree went to sleep, resolving to persuade Tom Fish to await developments. He believed they could find out through Fishing Bird just where and how the bloody trophy which was at the root of their difficulty, had been secured. That might throw great light on the problem.

John was early astir next morning and began preparations for the visit to the Indian town for the council meeting at which the bargain for their land was to be finally confirmed. Ree was strangely silent as he also arose and ate the breakfast which John had ready.

Tom Fish likewise had nothing to say except that he stated that he would remain at the cabin while the boys were away, and might be doing some work at chinking the walls.

It was in the early winter, but the day came out bright and clear. Greatly the boys enjoyed the bright sunshine and the bracing air as they took their way through the woods, crossing the river at last, and following a much used trail which took them toward the Delawares' village. This was a new route to them, but it was the course the Indians traveled and they found it better than the unbroken way they had previously taken in going to the lake beside which Capt. Pipe's people lived. As they walked along Ree told the story of Arthur Bridges as Tom had told it to him, and earnestly they discussed their situation.

In three hours the boys came to the Indian town, and Capt. Pipe called a council to settle the bargain for the land. There was speech making as before, but less of it, and then came a feast. But this too, was less formal than before. The Indians seemed about to go on a hunting expedition and had less time for other matters.

The Delawares promised to do much trading with the young Palefaces, and the boys would have considered their prospects very bright had it not been for the likelihood of trouble arising through Tom Fish's desire for revenge.

The little information Ree secured from Fishing Bird was not at all re-assuring, either. That agreeable, but none the less wily, savage would give him no satisfaction when he questioned him concerning the bloody trophy Big Buffalo had had, declaring, indeed, that no white man had been killed by the Delawares for a very long time.

The boys started on their homeward way in time to arrive before dark, and reached the clearing just after sundown. With a hop, step and jump John ran forward and up the ascent, to the door.

"Why, where is Tom?" he called as he entered. "The fire is out and there is no sign of him anywhere. He said he would stay here all day."

CHAPTER XIV.

Treed by Wolves.

The disappearance of Tom Fish caused both boys considerable uneasiness. They at first thought that he might return during the evening, though the fact that the fire had gone out, indicated that he had left the cabin early in the day. As they crept into their rough but comfortable bunks, however, and no sign of his coming had been heard, the lads realized the strong probability that the woodsman had set out by himself to avenge the death of Arthur Bridges, and that he had intended going when he told Ree the strange story of that young man, the night before.

What the consequences of Tom's undertaking might be, afforded grave cause for alarm. By reason of his having been looked upon as a member of their party, the Indians would consider the boys equally guilty in any offense which he might give.

"We will have to make the best of it, though and if it comes to fighting, we will fight like Trojans," said Ree, with some cheerfulness as he saw that John was quite depressed. "But our best plan will be to say nothing to Capt. Pipe's people about Tom. It may be that he left us on purpose to avoid getting us into trouble."

John agreed to this way of reasoning, hoping as Ree did, that it would be only a few days until they would see Tom and learn what his plans were. But time passed rapidly and nothing was seen or heard of the missing man. Had Tom been anything but a skilled woodsman the lads might probably have worried for his safety. As it was, that phase of the situation was scarcely thought of.

By working early and late, thawing the frozen clay beside their fire, when the weather was cold, that they might quickly get all the cracks in the cabin walls closed up, the boys accomplished a great deal in a week's time. Several times little parties of Indians came to trade with them, but the savages never mentioned Tom Fish's name. Big Buffalo came once and appeared more hateful than ever, suggesting the unpleasant thought that perhaps he knew more concerning the absent man than he would have been willing to tell.

The Delawares were not the only Indians who passed along the river and stopped to exchange skins for cloth, knives, beads or other articles. The Wyandots, Chippewas and Senecas had villages to the west and north and were coming or going quite frequently. Sometimes wandering Mingoes came along, and for them it may be said that they were more disposed to make trouble than any of the others. The reason probably lay in the fact that they were still to some extent influenced by British traders who retained feelings of hostility toward the colonies, and used their influence to secretly cause Indian disturbances along the borders.

At no great distance from the cabin was the Portage trail referred to in the previous chapter as passing near the Delaware town. This path was much used by all the Indians in traveling between the Great Lakes and the Ohio river, as it was the only stretch of land they must cross in making all the remainder of the journey by water. Thus they willingly carried their canoes over eight miles or so of land from the Cuyahoga to the Tuscarawas river, or vice versa, for the sake of paddling on their way with ease and rapidity the rest of the way, either north or south.

Thus, as their visitors were many, the loft the boys had built in their cabin came to contain a richer and richer store, as they placed there the furs they secured. Sitting before the fire at night they would sometimes estimate their probable profits, and as they discussed this and other subjects, the lads never forgot that their safety was the very first thing with which they must reckon. In this connection they were glad when they learned that Big Buffalo had gone away on a hunting trip with a large party of Delawares and would probably not return until spring.

There was another subject which was sometimes spoken of—the fact that the prowling enemy who had killed their horse had not for a long time given any sign of being in the vicinity. Out of these talks grew a theory that, perhaps, that secret foe was Big Pete Ellis, and that having killed old Jerry he had at last decided that his revenge was complete.

Their health, too, was a matter for daily thought with the boys, and remembering that they must be careful to guard against needless exposure, but both being hardy and robust, they were little troubled.

So the time passed and all promised well. They contrived many traps for the capture of fur-bearing animals, and to catch turkeys and other game for food. Chief of their traps was the dead-fall, made by propping up one end of a short piece of puncheon or hewed plank, in such a way that it would fall upon the animal which attempted to secure the bait placed on a trigger beneath it. This trigger was a part of the prop under the puncheon and gave way at the slightest jar. As the plank fell it caught the creature which had disturbed it, and being weighted down with stones, held its victim fast.

Wolf pens were also made and very successfully used. These were built of small logs on the same principle as a box trap, having a very heavy lid which fell, shutting inside any animal which entered and attempted to eat the bait placed on the spindle, which at the least pull, gave way, letting the lid fall.

The turkey traps were made in the Indian fashion. A small, low enclosure was built with sticks, a small opening or door being made close to the ground. The pen was then covered with brush except for a passage way leading to the door, and along this path beechnuts or other bait, were scattered, the trail of nuts extending into the enclosure. A turkey finding the food would follow it, its head near the ground, enter the pen, and having eaten all it could find, would raise its head and so be unable to see its way out.

The boys did not have so much time for hunting as they had planned upon, and yet scarcely a day passed but one of them sallied forth, nearly always coming home with valued furs or meat for their table. They found it advisable that one should remain near the cabin, both for its protection from Indians who might steal, and to trade with those who passed. Thus, while Ree would be spending a day with his axe clearing the land near their home, John would be miles away, perhaps, rifle in hand, eyes and ears alert.

The next day, perhaps, Ree would have his turn at hunting. Every day, too, they visited their traps to secure any creatures which had been captured and to reset the snares or change their location. Wood for the fire must be gathered, also, and it was wonderful how great a quantity of fuel the big fire-place consumed; and pine knots from the rocky ravine farther up the river, or hickory bark from the hillsides in the opposite direction, must be secured every few days to afford light for the evenings. There were also furs to be cured, and much else to be done, all uniting to make the short winter days very busy ones, and to keep the long winter evenings from being tedious.

Night was the favorite time for baking and for the preparation of such dishes as they thought they would most enjoy. Many were the feasts the young friends had, though their stock of supplies included little besides meal and fresh meat. At first they had occasionally secured beans and squashes from the Indians, but the improvident savages soon exhausted their supplies and were themselves dependent on corn and game.

December had gone and January was well under way when there came a great snow storm, which, at the end of a week left drifts piled high in all directions. The snow was soft and light but so deep that it was well nigh impossible for one to make his way through it, and Ree and John quickly agreed to occupy themselves with work in and near the cabin. They set about adding new conveniences to their home, such as shelves and cupboards, pegs, etc. They hewed and whittled out long, thin hickory slats, which they placed lengthwise on the rough bedstead they had built in one corner, and found them so springy and comfortable to sleep upon, when a couple of skins and a blanket had been spread over them, that they were sorry they had not sooner thought of this improvement.

John made a broom of hickory splints which did its work to perfection, and Ree sharpened up his knife and carved from a whitewood block several plates and trays to add to their meager collection of dishes. Both boys improved the opportunity also, while shut in, to give their wardrobes attention, making themselves stout moccasins, coon-skin caps and buckskin breeches.

Ree found time during many evenings to read again and again the few books he had. John was less given to reading, but with much care and diligence he managed to make a fife by boring a maple stick through from end to end with a thin piece of iron from their cart, much of which had been carried piece-meal to the cabin. Having natural musical talent, he learned to play the instrument he thus fashioned, and though Ree had declared, as he practiced, that he would surely bring the savages down upon them in war paint, he liked the music as well as its maker.

So, for a fortnight the boys were scarcely out of sight of the cabin. The weather was bitter cold much of that time and no Indians came near. There at last came a day, however, when the wind blew steadily from the southwest, bringing with it at night a cold rain. Changing to the north, the wind turned the rain to sleet, followed by cold weather again.

"We must have snow-shoes," said Ree, when he saw what was taking place, and the third day the boys ventured forth on such contrivances as they had made and did finely with them on the thick, slippery crust which had formed. Taking their rifles, they made their way through the river valley, which, farther up the stream, became quite narrow, steep, rocky banks rising on both sides to a height of fifty feet or more. No sooner had they entered this canyon than they found evidences of deer and other animals having taken shelter there.

Going quietly forward, the lads discovered four of the timid, beautiful creatures huddled together. They went quite near before the deer leaped away through the frozen snow, and Ree quickly brought one down. John did better—or worse— killing one and wounding another. They secured the skins and choice parts of the meat and hanging these in a tree for safety, pushed on after the two which had escaped. They especially desired to capture the doe which had been wounded, not so much for its value, but because Ree insisted that it would be downright cruelty to let the poor creature suffer from its injury for days, perhaps, then die at last.

But the young hunters traveled far before again coming upon the animals they sought. The trail took them out of the narrow valley or canyon, and a long distance through the woods to a locality they had never before visited, where the earth was cut by deep ravines, zig-zagging in nearly all directions, and great rocks often obstructing the way. Here the trail of the deer they were following was lost amid the tracks of others which had gone into the deep rugged gullies to escape the stinging wind.

"We may as well give it up, Ree," said John, as they sat down to rest.

"Oh no, we mustn't give up," Ree answered, "but I'll tell you what we'd better do. It is more than likely the Indians will be out in snow shoes the same as we are, and they may want to swap some dollar furs for penny knick-knacks this afternoon. One of us should be at the cabin."

"I'll go," John willingly responded, for he liked to trade with the Indians, and could make much better bargains than Ree; not but what he was honest, but because Ree was so generous that he was often imposed upon.

"Will you stop for the venison we left in the tree?" Ree asked.

"I think I'd better; there is no knowing where you will be when you find that wounded deer! But don't stay out all night!"

With this sally John started homeward, and Ree resumed his search for blood-stains in the snow which would show him the trail he sought. Going about among the rocks he discovered an opening about half the size of a door which seemed to lead straight back into a rocky cliff.

"Some sort of a cave," he mused, inspecting it more closely and looking into it. He saw nothing, and, stooping down, ventured in a little way. His eyes accustomed to the bright light of the snow, he was unable to see anything in the darkness, or he might not have been so bold; for the next moment a chorus of fierce growls caused him to retreat.

"Bears, or wolves—bears, most likely," said Ree to himself. "At least if they are wolves there should be tracks about the mouth of the cave. I must remember this place."

Having first looked about to make sure of the exact location of the cavern, and resolving to explore it at some future time, the youthful hunter hurried on. Under a clump of low pines he presently discovered a herd of seven deer. One lagged behind, as they fled at his approach, and Ree knew at once that it must be the wounded animal. He followed at the best pace possible, but the deer was soon lost sight of, though the poor thing had a difficult time of it to make any progress through the crusted snow.

However, Ree kept to the trail for he was sure the doe could not go far; yet hour after hour passed and he saw no hope of accomplishing his purpose. Had it not been that the deer was traversing a circle, the trail now taking him in the direction of the cabin, he would have been obliged to give up the pursuit. But now he passed through the ravine where the deer had been wounded and up a steep slope towards home. By this time the sun was going down, and from not far ahead of him Ree heard the howling of wolves. If he could have looked but a little way into the future, he would have taken the shortest route to the cabin.

However, wolves had never given much trouble and Ree had no thought of being afraid, though the howling sounded nearer and nearer as he continued on. Soon, however, he guessed what had happened. The wounded deer, unable to escape, had been killed by the fierce dogs of the wilderness which were now devouring it. And in another minute the boy saw them at their awful feast. With anger and foolhardy courage he sprang directly among the struggling beasts, clubbing them with his rifle.

Mad with starvation and the taste of fresh blood, one big wolf leaped toward the courageous boy and others followed. He was barely able to hold them at bay while he backed away toward a tree, swinging his rifle right and left with desperate energy as he went. Closer and closer still the wolves pressed him, snapping, snarling, howling—their long sharp teeth and red throats being so near that he could almost feel their hot breath on his face. But he reached the tree—a beech, one of whose lower limbs was almost within reach. He leaped upward to seize it, but as he did so his rifle caught on a bush and was jerked from his hand. A great gray foamy-jawed creature snapped closely at his heels and by a hair's breadth he escaped, as he drew himself quickly upward.

Howling like enraged demons the wolves gathered about the tree. They seemed to know that sooner or later they would drink human blood. Ree thought of this. His only weapon was the knife Capt. Bowen had given him, which he always carried. But his active brain was busy and he determined to take a desperate chance in an effort to secure his rifle.

CHAPTER XV.

A Maple Sugar Camp in the Wilderness.

Selecting a stout limb for his purpose, Ree set to work to cut and trim it, making a short, heavy club. He believed that if he should jump suddenly down among the wolves, their surprise would be so great as to keep them away for perhaps a second—long enough to permit him to seize his rifle, and again fight his way into the tree. As he trimmed the thick branch, however, an increasing danger presented itself. The unusual howling of the pack and the scent of blood were attracting other wolves to the spot. Before his club was ready, he had counted seven newcomers galloping through the snow to join their blood-thirsty brothers.

To put his life in peril by jumping down among so many of the fierce creatures was to run a greater risk than Ree thought wise; but his fertile brain presented a new plan. He partially split one end of his club and securely bound the handle of the knife in the opening thus made, with strips of buckskin cut from his clothing. In this way he made a strong but cumbersome spear, and holding to the lowest branch of the tree, he leaned far down and stabbed and slashed at every wolf within reach.

Several were wounded and their yelps of pain and rage were added to the hideous, hungry cries of the others. Again and again the bold boy cut and thrust as the wolves kept coming within his reach. The snow was dyed with blood. For half an hour the battle was carried on.

At last by a lucky stroke Ree gave one of the howling mass beneath him so deep a cut across the neck, that it sprang but a few yards away and fell dead, its head half cut off. At once the others pounced upon the wolf's body, tearing it to pieces, scrambling and fighting in a most horrible manner.

Now was Ree's chance. He leaped quickly to the ground and seized his blood-stained rifle; in another moment he would have been safe. But he was so chilled—so stiff from the cold, that he missed his hold when first he sprang to catch the lowest branch, and before he could try again, a monstrous gray wolf dashed toward him. With a hungry howl, its jaws dripping blood, it launched itself through the air, straight for Ree's throat.

With wonderful nerve the boy stood his ground. He did not falter, nor hesitate. He met the hot-mouthed, vicious brute, his rude spear clasped in both hands, and drove the blade deep in its shaggy shoulder. With an almost human shriek and ferocity the wolf sprang sidewise under the impulse of the steel's sharp thrust, and the spear quivering in its flesh, was jerked from the boys' hands.

Ree's first impulse was to run in pursuit, as the wolf dashed into the woods, to recover his knife; but in an instant the whole pack was upon him again, having made short work of their cannibal-like feast, and only by the greatest dexterity was he able again to seize his rifle and climb to safety, ere they reached him.

"Now some of you will smart!" the half-frozen boy exclaimed, and he clenched his teeth in righteous anger. Shot after shot he poured into the blood-thirsty brutes, and watched with horror as those remaining alive pounced upon the dying ones. Four wolves he killed and two he wounded, then sat still awhile to catch his breath and scrutinize the dozen animals remaining, to see whether the one in whose body his knife had been carried off, was there. He did not see it, though the twilight gloom was now dispelled by bright moonlight. So, soon he resumed the terrible execution he had wrought among the pack, and was firing as fast as he could load, when he heard John's familiar whistle.

"Watch out, John! There are still eight of the fiercest wolves you ever saw here!" he called in warning, but almost simultaneously his chum's rifle sounded, and but seven wolves remained. Another and another went down to death and the five which were left, taking fright at last, sped away among the timber, howling dismally.

"You had me scared into fits, almost," John cried, as Ree climbed down. "Why, how cold you are!" he exclaimed, grasping his friend's hand. "And your teeth are chattering! How did it happen any way? Come along home!"

"I'll tell you about it; but we'd better skin the wolves that have not been half eaten, first. Bloody as a battle field, isn't it?"

"Skin nothing! Come along! It is most terribly cold and you are half frozen. We can get the skins in the morning if there is any thing left of them."

For once Ree yielded and when he had recovered his snow-shoes John marched him off at a pace which soon put his blood in circulation.

If ever the young pioneers appreciated the rude comforts of their cabin, they did that night. It was sweet to feel snug and warm and safe, as Ree told the story of his adventure more fully than at first; to stretch their weary legs toward the crackling fire and lean back in the fur covered seat they had constructed. It was pleasant to eat a lunch of nuts secured from the Indians, and venison steaks cut thin and broiled crisp. It was comfortable to creep into bed and lie awake and talk of their plans; of their friends in far away Connecticut; of incidents of their trip; of the strange absence of Tom Fish; of the sad story of Arthur Bridges—of many, many things.

And it was pleasant to watch with half closed eyes, the firelight dancing on the rough cabin walls, shining in the little looking glass near the door, showing the rifles within easy reach in the corner near the bed; the two sets of pistols in their hostlers on the table they had made; the gleaming blades of their axes, beside the fire-place; the books Ree loved so well, arranged on a board from the old cart, which did duty as a mantel, and John's fife beside them; the frying-pan and their few dishes on and in a little cupboard in the corner. It was sweet, too, to fall asleep at last and dream of the present, past and future—enjoying the perfect rest which the fatigue of honest, hard work by those possessed of honest hearts must ever bring.

The boys were very tired this night, partly from the unusual exercise of walking so far on snow-shoes, no doubt. But they slept soundly and were early awake. Directly after breakfast they visited the scene of the fight with the wolves. They little expected to find anything left of their victims, excepting bones, but they greatly desired to find the knife which had been Capt. Bowen's present.

Bones they did find—but nothing else. There was every evidence of a ghastly feast having been eaten by the wolves and other animals during the night. Even the skeletons of those which had been slaughtered, were torn to pieces, and for rods around the snow was dyed crimson.

To cry over spilled milk was no part of Ree's disposition, and though he deeply regretted the loss of his knife, he did not allow himself to be dispirited, though little he thought how important a part in their adventures the knife was yet to play.

In their walks about the woods at different times, Ree and John had observed that there were many sugar maples near their cabin and had agreed that they must make some sugar when spring came. That very afternoon, therefore, they began preparations.

Blocks of wood, cut into lengths of about two feet, they hollowed out with their axes, making troughs in which to catch the sap of maples. The work was tedious and many a trough was split and spoiled when all but completed, before they caught the knack of avoiding this by striking curved strokes with their axes, and not letting the blades cut in deeply, in line with the grain of the wood.

This work, and the making of spouts by punching the pith out of sumac branches occupied several days. Not all their time could be given to it, however, as traps must be visited and Indians given attention; for now that the weather was becoming warm the savages came frequently, often with many furs secured during winter hunting expeditions.

"We have made a pretty good living and a nice sum of money for each of us, when our furs shall have been marketed, and have also made ourselves a home," said Ree one day, as they were estimating the probable value of their stores. "After deducting for all losses, we will still have done splendidly if we are fortunate in getting the skins to Pittsburg or Detroit and working a fair bargain with the buyers."

"We better get a good canoe Ree, and learn to use it; then we can take the furs from here to Detroit by water, traveling along the shore of Lake Erie," John suggested. "Capt. Pipe has a couple of fine, big canoes of his own, buried for the winter. I believe he would sell us one."

"We will go and have a talk with him about it soon," Ree answered. But it was not for many days that the lads found time to do this.

Fine weather came sooner than they expected. The spring of 1791 was one of the earliest known to the section which is now Northern Ohio. Even in February the sun came out bright and warm and the cold winds disappeared.

John and Ree awoke one morning after a rainy night to find the water high in the river, the ice gone and the air as mild as on a day in May.

"Hooray! I've a mind to take a swim!" John shouted, looking with enthusiasm at the high water.

"I wish we had our canoe now," Ree joined in; "but I'll tell you, old chap, we must get our maples tapped, if we are to get any sugar."

John turned away from watching the swift, deep current with a sigh. Somehow he did not feel like working; but under Ree's influence he soon forgot his "spring fever" feeling, and with a small auger bored holes in the trees. Into these holes Ree drove the spouts, placing a trough beneath each one, to catch the sap which at once began to flow.

As all the trees were near the cabin the boys might have carried the sap to their fire-place for boiling, but as this would necessitate the carrying of a great deal of wood, they hung their largest kettle on a pole laid across two forked sticks driven in the ground for that purpose, just at the top of the hill near the edge of the clearing.

By noon enough sap was collected in the troughs to make it necessary to begin the boiling, and from then on through all that day and the next, one of the boys was constantly busy, keeping the fire blazing hot and gathering sap to keep the kettle well filled, as the water was boiled away, leaving only its sweetness. At last they added no fresh sap but allowed the syrup in the kettle to boil down thicker and thicker making in the end, most delicious molasses.

The boys finished the boiling in the cabin that night, and when the syrup had become thick enough, they were able by stirring and cooling it, to make an excellent quality of sugar. And it had been so long since either of them had tasted sweets, that the maple's fine product was indeed a treat. The prospect that they would be able to make enough sugar to last them until another spring, was highly agreeable, and they were willing enough to work hard during many days which followed.

One regret the boys had, was that they possessed but two kettles, neither of which was very large; but they boiled sap in both and found that by greasing the upper edges of the vessels that they could keep them quite full and still the sap would not boil over.

They also tried the very primitive method used by the Indians before they had kettles in which to make sugar. Several large, nearly round stones were washed clean, then heated very hot in the fire. With improvised tongs they were then lifted into a large keg of cold sap. As this operation was constantly repeated, the sap was heated and slowly evaporated.

The process proved so very slow and laborious, however, that the boys soon abandoned it. But while the experiment was being tried, something occurred which made John laugh until he held his sides. The keg of sap had been heated to almost a boiling point, and putting a couple of large, hot stones in it both boys left the camp, John to gather more sap and Ree to chop some wood.

As John was returning, he discovered a young bear prowling about the camp. The animal evidently had not been long out of its winter quarters and was hungry. It sniffed the sweet odor which came from the evaporating maple water, and ambled up to the keg.

Quietly John ran and called Ree, and they both hurried softly back just as the bear put its nose deep into the hot sap. A squeal of pain followed, and the poor cub nearly turned a backward somersault, with such sudden energy did it take its nose out of the keg. Wild with the smarting burns the creature rushed blindly about, almost burying its head in the cool leaves and earth, and missing its footing, somehow, as it approached a steep part of the hill, fell and rolled to the bottom, squealing and growling woefully. Before John could check his laughter, the bear had picked itself up and trotted swiftly away, and Ree was willing to let it go unharmed, though he could have shot it.

This incident set the boys to thinking. Bruin evidently knew the smell of honey better than of sap. All bears delight in sweet things, and Ree said he had no doubt there were bee trees in the neighborhood. At any rate, the lads decided, it would be well worth while to be on the lookout for them as they were about the woods during the spring and summer.

Continued fine weather put an end to the maple season. In a fortnight the buds began to open on the trees and the flow of sap ceased. About this time, too, the Portage trail, not far away, was constantly traversed by redskins, many of them strangers, and there were daily calls at the cabin of the young Palefaces. So there was much to do; the spring crops must be planted, the pile of furs must be taken to market and fences must be completed to keep deer and other animals out of the cornfield they proposed having.

There was another thing needing early attention, and that was the securing of land at the junction of the Portage trail and the river. For the boys could not but see how advantageous that place would be as a trading point, and they wished to build a new and larger cabin there. Moreover, as the country was opened up and settled, the land about so favorable a site for a town would probably become very valuable.

"We will go to see Capt. Pipe to-morrow, and bargain with him for a canoe, and for some land where the trail and the river meet," said Ree one warm March night as they sat on the doorstep of their cabin, in the moonlight.

CHAPTER XVI.

The Hatred of Big Buffalo.

The last of the sap had been reduced to sugar and made into a fine solid cake weighing nearly two pounds, the night that the foregoing conversation took place. With this as a present to the chief of the Delawares, Ree and John set out early the following morning for Capt. Pipe's town on the lake.

It was a beautiful day. The red buds on the trees were bursting into green, in places, and in many sunny spots the spring plants and flowers were shooting forth. All nature seemed to feel the same joy and freedom the young pioneers felt as they journeyed through the valley and over the hills toward their destination. Birds were singing on every hand. Crows were flying here and there and calling lustily to one another from all directions.

Once a young deer bounded toward the boys, then, after standing for a moment, gazing with great, timid, bright eyes, wheeled and was away again, springing over bushes and logs with a showy vigor as though it were out only for a spring frolic. A wild turkey hen, wandering about in search of a place for nesting, scampered softly out of sight as it caught sight of the lads. A big woodchuck, fat and lazy, even after its all-winter nap, circled around a tree, to whose trunk it was clinging, thinking, perhaps, that it was always keeping just out of sight of the human intruders upon its forest home, though it was badly fooled if such were its opinion. A dozen times either boy could have shot it had he been so disposed.

A myriad of ducks flew noisily from a stream near the lake in which they were feeding as John threw a stone among them. He and Ree could have killed a score of the wild fowls had they wished to do so, but they were in no mood for it. They had not set out to hunt, and moreover, the fresh, balmy air and invigorating sunlight, together with the delightful odors of the spring-time, put upon them both a spell—a joy in living which made it seem inhuman to harm any living creature that day.

This sense of gladness, of friendship with every thing the woods contained, did not, however, prevent the boys from laying plans for the capture of certain denizens of the forest's waters—the fish. They had already noticed that the lake beside which the Delawares lived, also other lakes not far away, and their own river, contained great numbers of the finny tribe, but they had been too busy with other things to try their hands at fishing. The opportunity for this fine sport, however, caused them to deeply regret that they had brought nothing in the line of fishing tackle with them.

"The Indians will surely have hooks, and spears, though," John suggested.

"If they haven't, we can make nets and spears too; I shouldn't be surprised if we could contrive hooks as well," Ree answered.

"I wish we had a big mess of fish for dinner!" John exclaimed. "I'm hungry as a bear."

His wish was realized sooner than he expected. As was their custom, the Indians at once placed food before their visitors, and the fare was just what John had wanted. There was one objection—the savages cooked the fish without cutting off the heads, but the boys did this for themselves. That they could not be over-particular in the wilderness, they had long since discovered.

They learned that the Delawares had caught the fish with hooks made of bones— evidently small wish-bones, and readily saw how they could make just such hooks for themselves.

Capt. Pipe himself had received the boys, and it was in his lodge that they were eating. He sat nearby gravely smoking his pipe, seldom speaking except when spoken to. Gentle Maiden, the chief's comely daughter, was sitting in a pleasant, sunny place just outside the bark hut, sewing with a coarse bone needle, on some sort of a frock, the cloth for which was from the bolt her father had secured from the young traders.

"Pretty as a picture, isn't she?" John whispered, glancing toward the Indian girl. "Honestly, I never saw a white person more beautiful."

Ree made no reply, for at that moment Big Buffalo put his head into the lodge. The boys had not seen him since early winter and both arose to greet him; but he ignored their action, and pausing only a second, strode haughtily away.

"What does that mean?" John asked in surprise.

"Has the Big Buffalo cause to be unfriendly?" inquired Ree of Capt. Pipe, wishing to call the chief's attention to the Indian's apparent hostility.

"Buffalo heap big fool," Capt. Pipe grunted, and then in the Delaware tongue he spoke to his daughter, and she arose and took a seat inside the lodge, behind her father.

This incident filled Ree with misgiving though he was not sure enough that he had cause for such feeling to mention it at that time. John was differently impressed.

"Why," he exclaimed, "Big Buffalo is on a mighty high horse to-day! He acts like a child that has been told it must wait till second table at a dinner! I wonder if there is any love lost between him and the Gentle Maiden?" he added in a whisper.

Ree did not answer, but now that they had finished dinner, signified their wish to talk to Capt. Pipe about buying a canoe.

The chief said he would make a trade with them and asked what the boys had to give. In return they asked to see the craft he proposed swapping, and were then conducted to a hillside where a canoe had but recently been dug out of the dry muck and earth in which it was buried over winter to save it from drying, cracking or warping.

Ree and John examined the frail boat of bitter-nut hickory bark, with much interest. It was about eleven feet in length, well constructed, and water-tight. With it were a couple of light, nicely carved paddles.

John promptly pronounced the canoe a "regular macaroni" and laid down a pair of brass buckles, signifying that he would give them for the skiff.

Capt. Pipe gravely shook his head.

"I'll add this," said Ree, and laid down a brand new hunting knife, having a leather sheath.

The chief again shook his head, and a large number of Indians, who had been lazily basking in the sun or idly paddling about the lake, and were now gathered around to see the trade, also shook their heads.

"The thing isn't worth as much as we have offered," cried John, good humoredly, "but I'll put in this," and he produced a large yellow silk handkerchief, shaking it out, and holding it up to view in an attractive manner.

Still Capt. Pipe shook his head and all his braves did the same, though their eyes glistened.

Ree hesitated before adding more to their offer and while he did so, John picked up the handkerchief and with no thought but to display it to good advantage, turned to Gentle Maiden, who stood at her father's side. With a quiet sweep of his hand he draped the bright cloth over the girl's shoulder and arm.

The next instant a stinging blow struck him in the face and he staggered, nearly falling. It was Big Buffalo's fist that had shot out at him.

John sprang toward the burly Indian and they grappled in a terrible struggle. All had taken place so quickly that before Ree could reach John's side, his friend's throat was in the redman's grasp and the breath squeezed nearly out of him. Capt. Pipe also rushed in, and amid the yells of the Indians, the chief and Ree soon separated the combatants.

The incident created so much excitement that the young Palefaces scarcely knew what to do. But Ree's firm voice and quiet dignity, as he told the chief that his friend had meant no offense, and should not have been assaulted, had a quieting influence on the savages, and although John could scarcely refrain from speaking the angry words he thought, he did manage to hold his tongue, and Capt. Pipe soon restored order.

Big Buffalo slunk away like a whipped dog, as the chief berated him, and the boys saw no more of him that day. How much better it would have been had they never seen him again!

The bargain for the canoe was completed by Ree adding a second handkerchief to their offer, as much as a peace offering as anything, and then as it was growing late, and the disturbance had made the question of buying more land a dangerous one to be brought up, at that time, the boys departed. They shook hands with

Capt. Pipe and the braves standing near, and Fishing Bird went with them as they carried their canoe down to the water and launched it.

While pretending to show the lads about handling the canoe, this friendly Indian warned them to watch out for Big Buffalo; that he supposed them to be admirers of Gentle Maiden, with whom he was in love, and would kill them if he got a chance. Moreover, that he had set out to kill them when they first arrived and would have done so but through fear of Capt. Pipe with whom they had made peace.

The information Fishing Bird imparted, with the exception of the latter part, was no news to the boys; but it was so disquieting that instead of paddling about the lake until evening, as they had intended, they crossed the water, carried their canoe overland to the river, and went directly home.

John was very blue over what had occurred, blaming himself for having caused the trouble. Ree was not so much depressed. His nature was not one of extremes; he was never hilariously merry, never completely dejected.

"It was no more your fault than my own, John," said he, as they talked of Big Buffalo's display of malice. "You meant no harm, and if the ugly fellow had not hated us to start with, he would not have taken offense so easily. We may have some trouble with him, and again we may not. Capt. Pipe will be on our side, I'm sure, for you heard what the chief said about the rascal. The fact is, that in spite of all the stories we have heard about Capt. Pipe and his cruelty, he has certainly been friendly with us, and honest."

By talking in this way Ree restored John to a happier mood, and they were both quite jolly again as they prepared and ate their supper. They looked forward to many happy days in their canoe on the lake and river, and John proposed to rig up a sail with the canvas which had been over their cart, and by doing so to give the Indians quite a surprise.

That evening the boys turned their attention to making spears for fishing. They used some seasoned hickory which Ree had put in the loft during the winter for the making of bows, and were able to whittle stout, sharp prongs out of that hard, tough wood. It was too late when the task was completed, however, to try the spears that night, but the boys went to bed promising themselves good sport the next evening.

Although it was still the month of March, the early spring of that year enabled the young pioneers to begin at once active preparations for planting corn, potatoes, beans and squashes. The brush cut during the winter was so dry that it burned readily, and the green brush was easily disposed of also, when piled upon the hot fires the dry wood made. In this way the natural clearing was soon rid of the scattered undergrowth upon it.

In a week or two the boys were ready to put the seed into the ground, digging up a space a foot square wherever they planted a hill of beans, corn, potatoes or squashes. It was slow work, nevertheless, and the sturdy, youthful farmers were obliged to toil early and late.

The coming of Indians frequently interrupted the boys at their work, and they came at last to continue their labor after greeting their visitors, unless the latter wished to trade. This the redmen liked none too well. They seemed to think their Paleface neighbors were devoting too much time to agricultural pursuits, and they feared and hated any and all things which threatened to turn their forests into farm lands. But Ree and John agreed that, since they had bought the land of the Indians, they might as well give the former owners to understand, first and last, that they meant to do with it as they liked.

Big Buffalo was among a party which stopped at the cabin one day. He refused food and made himself generally disagreeable. The boys, however, ignored his ill humor and by paying no attention to him, showed that they neither cared for his hatred nor feared him, even though they knew there was murder in his heart.

Frequently strange Indians were among those who called and they asked the boys to visit their towns, some of which were not many miles away, to trade. As all of those Indians traversed the Portage trail or path, the boys were reminded almost daily of the desirability of securing land for a trading post, at the junction of the trail and the river. As they talked the matter over and looked into the future, more and more did they regret that the violent conduct of Big Buffalo had prevented their prolonging their bargaining with Capt. Pipe on the occasion of their last visit to him.

About this time, also, another reason arose for the two friends wishing to visit Capt. Pipe again. It was the discovery that he had secured some horses. During the winter he had had none of which the boys knew. Now, they reasoned, if they could buy a horse, they would rig up their cart and carry their furs to Pittsburg. It would be a much shorter and safer trip than to undertake to reach Detroit, and they would require no assistance. There was some probability, too, that among their friends in Pittsburg they might get some word concerning Tom Fish.

It was one night when they had returned from fishing, bringing in a great string of rock bass, that the lads talked this over, and at last concluded to go again to the Delaware town, even at the risk of having more trouble with Big Buffalo.

It seemed like a holiday after their hard work when, next day, the boys found themselves in their canoe, gliding over the river's rippling waters on their way to Capt. Pipe's home. They carried the craft overland to the lake and soon approached the Indian village.

But suddenly as they drew near, the noise of many voices was borne to them by the breeze. First loud, then low, the sounds came across the water. Ree's face grew grave, and John, who had been whistling, abruptly paused.

"Ree," he exclaimed, "that is the song of the war dance!"

"It means that the Indians are going on the warpath, as surely as we hear it," was the answer. "Be on your guard, John. We will soon find out just what it means; for we won't turn back now, even if we see the whole tribe in war paint."

CHAPTER XVII.

Danger.

As Ree spoke, a war whoop sounded clear and strong, instantly followed by a weird, chanting song. In a minute or two this ceased, and then with fiercer war whoops than before, broke out afresh. Quickly the young pioneers floated nearer the scene of these warlike outbursts, and soon ran the nose of their canoe upon the gravelly beach. With fast-beating hearts they climbed the little bank which rose gradually a few feet back from the shore.

The boys had approached so quietly, and the Indians were so intent on the war dance that their coming had not been discovered. And well might the lads pause in uncertainty as to the manner of the reception they would receive; for now they came into full view of the assembled savages—half-naked warriors in paint and fighting costume, forming a circle and dancing and yelling like the wild barbarians they were, while old men and young braves and squaws and children looked on in savage rapture. Before either boy could speak Big Buffalo espied them and leaped forward brandishing a tomahawk.

Instinctively Ree seized his rifle in both hands, ready for instant action. John did the same, and with an ugly leer the Indian paused. His action had attracted attention, however, and at this critical juncture Capt. Pipe discovered the presence of the visitors, and called angrily to Buffalo to put up his weapon.

The chief was in full war costume himself, making anything but a peaceable appearance as he met the boys half way, when they obeyed his signal to approach.

But without a word he conducted them to a place in the circle of spectators gathered around the forty or fifty warriors, and at once the dance went on as though there had been no interruption.

With terrible gestures of their arms and throwing their bodies into all sorts of warlike attitudes, the Indians danced about in a circle, striking their feet down with great force as they kept time to the beating of two rude drums and the uncanny song they sang. With a war whoop a dance was begun and continued for about two minutes, the outlandish music making the forest ring. Then the singing and dancing stopped and the Indians walked more slowly around the circle.

In a minute or so another war-cry would sound and the fierce, weird music and dance would be resumed. Then some old Indian among the spectators would clap his hands, signifying that he wished to speak. The dance would cease and the dancers walk slowly 'round again, while a speech was made. The address would occupy only a half minute or a minute perhaps, and then with another of the horrifying war cries the dancing and singing were started afresh.

Ree and John might have been a thousand miles away for all the attention that was given them at first.

"Perhaps it is merely a festival dance," John whispered to his chum.

"No, it would be given in the evening if that were true," was the answer. "It means the warpath, I am sure."

John was replying that, whether merely for entertainment or for war, the dance was enough to scare a civilized person into a trance, when Capt. Pipe suddenly clapped his hands and, as the music ceased, stepped forward and spoke. All the other speeches had been made in the Delaware tongue, but the first man of the tribe now spoke partly in English. This was for the purpose of giving them to understand just what was going on, the boys were quite certain, and frequently the chief pointed toward them.

In substance Capt. Pipe said that the whites were encroaching too far upon the lands of the Indians and preparations were being made for a great union of tribes to drive the "Long Knives" back. He promised to lead a large party of his people to join with other Delawares and the Wyandots, Shawnees and Miamies in a war which, he boastfully said, would secure to the Indians again the forests in which the Palefaces had already settled. He referred to the defeat of the whites eight years before and the burning of Col. Crawford, and said there would be scalps and plunder for every warrior who accompanied him.

John found himself wondering whether the Indians might not undertake to whet their appetites for blood by killing himself and Ree. It was of the terrible torture of Col. Crawford which Ree was thinking, and he found it hard to keep from hating the savages before him, horrible and cruel in their war paint.

And could he have looked but a few months into the future and have seen the awful carnage in which Capt. Pipe and his braves had a prominent part, at the defeat of General St. Clair near Fort Jefferson, in what is now Mercer County, Ohio, he could not have restrained his hatred as he did. He knew in after years what that battle was, and knew that the Indians boasted that their arms ached from their work with the scalping knife.

The frightful dance went on when Capt. Pipe had finished speaking, his words inspiring the warriors with new vigor who now whirled around the circle with great rapidity, going through all the motions of attacking, vanquishing and scalping an enemy. At a call from the chief, other warriors, who were standing by, sprang into the ring, joining in the singing and contortions of faces and bodies with furious energy. More and more followed as from among the dancers Capt. Pipe called from time to time, urging all who wished to win renown as warriors, and to hang scalps of the hated whites at their belts, to join him.

Each addition to the whirling, shrieking, blood-thirsty band was greeted with thunderous whoops and in the end nearly one hundred and fifty braves were going through all the barbarous awe-inspiring motions of the horrid celebration.

Well might Ree and John feel alarm for their own safety; but they looked upon the terrifying scene quite calmly, notwithstanding that, as their passions were kindled and their savage patriotism aroused by the fervor of the dance, the Indians gave them many a glance which was far from friendly.

There were two things which Ree could not help but notice as the revel continued; one was that Big Buffalo had not joined the dancers, the other that Gentle Maiden kept her eyes downcast or looked away across the lake, not once turning toward her father's painted braves. He could not help thinking it strange that the Buffalo had not signified his intention of joining the warriors, and sincerely wished the unfriendly fellow had done so. There was no other Indian whom he had so much reason to dislike, nor one whose absence was so greatly to be desired.

For more than two hours the dance went on, interrupted only when some one—usually an old Indian whose fighting days were past—clapped his hands as a signal that he wished to make a speech. But at last Capt. Pipe called a halt and stepped out from among the dancers. With a fierce look toward Big Buffalo he demanded to know of him why he would not join the war party.

Ree and John could not understand all that was said, but they saw plainly that the chief was angry. In substance the reason of Big Buffalo was that it would not do for all the strong men to leave the village; that some one must remain to provide meat for the women and children, and to protect the town.

Capt. Pipe heard these excuses with a scowl black as a thunder cloud. His giant frame stretched itself to its greatest height and his voice was filled with contempt as he flung forth but one word:

"Squaw!"

Perhaps the chief thought, as Ree was at that moment thinking, that the Buffalo's main reason for wishing to remain at home, was that he might be near Gentle Maiden. But had the truth been made known, it would have been shown that the treacherous rascal had other and more wicked reasons in his heart, as the young settlers were destined soon to learn.

With a wave of his arm Capt. Pipe dispersed his followers as Big Buffalo made no reply to his contemptuous outburst. The Indians threw themselves on the ground to rest, or went away to their lodges to more fully prepare for the warpath, and the chief, turning to Ree and John, motioned to them to follow. He led the boys to his cabin and his wife placed food before them. When they had eaten, Capt. Pipe produced pipes and all three smoked. It was a silent compact of peace, and pleased indeed were the Paleface lads that the Indian showed this disposition.

Though it was not this act of friendship which made him bold, for he would have spoken in the same way under other circumstances, Ree quietly asked Capt. Pipe why he had determined to go on the warpath.

The chief made no answer.

"It is wrong," Ree continued gravely. "You are living here in happiness and security. No Palefaces have molested you. Your people are contented; they have but to step into the forests for an abundance of game; but to approach the waters for all the fish they may desire. The ground yields rich returns from the labor of the planting season. The Delawares are well fed and well clothed. Why, then, should they give up the hunt and the pleasures of their present pursuits to take up the hatchet? Why should they seek the lives of others, whether white men or redmen?

They will only bring sorrow and weeping to their own villages, and sorrow and weeping in many a Paleface home for those who never return. More than this, Chief Hopocon, the Great Spirit looks with unhappy eyes upon his children who go on the warpath not in defense of their own, but to kill and murder those who have not harmed them."

Knowing Ree even well as he did, John was surprised to hear him speak thus fluently and strongly, but he greatly feared his friend had been unwise in speaking so boldly.

For a few seconds Capt. Pipe did not answer. And then he said:

"The young brother speaks well, but he does not know. His heart is right, but he does not know. With the young men who have come among us as traders and hunters we have no quarrel. They will remain here. They will send no word of the war dance to the forts. Other Palefaces are crowding further and further. Faster and faster, they are driving the people of the forest before them. The young brother does not know this. The young brother does not know of the word which every day the runners bring, which tells of the crowding of the Long Knives more and more upon the forest. Now must they be warned to come no further. Now must they be driven back to the eastward. Else the setting sun will be the home of the Delawares. Too long—too long, have the hands of Hopocon and his warriors been idle; too long—too long, have the Delawares borne in silence."

Capt. Pipe spoke with emphasis but not violently. As he concluded he rose slowly to his feet. Ree and John followed his example, and with meaning in his gesture far greater than words could have expressed, the chieftain motioned to them to depart.

With shoulders thrown back, head erect as proud and dignified as the Indians whom he felt had thus insulted him Ree turned to leave the cabin. But John had no such feeling, nor was he so quick to see that Capt. Pipe was offended by the words of one whom he probably considered a mere boy. He saw only that the object of their visit was not likely to be accomplished and turning to the Indian said: "Capt. Pipe, we wanted to buy a little more land, and we need a horse."

With an impatient, violent sweep of his right hand, the chief touched John's shoulder with his left, and pointed across the lake in the direction of the cabin by the river.

Even in this brief time Ree's temper had cooled, and with proud dignity he turned and offered Capt. Pipe his hand. The Indian took it and also shook hands with

John. His manner was haughty but not altogether unfriendly. The boys still felt that they had nothing to fear from him as they walked away.

Fishing Bird was near by as usual, as the lads went down to the water's edge. He was naked to the waist and was bedecked with paint and feathers. He looked really fierce as he strode up to shove off the canoe, not in his customary happy mood, but with cool indifference. He spoke to Ree in an undertone as the canoe glided free of the beach.

It was late in the day, and this fact taken in connection with the unpleasant events of the afternoon caused the boys to decide to go directly to their cabin rather than to go on to the Tuscarawas river upon which the Indians were accustomed to travel toward the Ohio, and which the lads had planned to explore.

"What did Fishing Bird say to you, Ree?" asked John as they reached mid-lake.

"He said we should watch out for Big Buffalo."

"Thunderation! I wonder if he isn't jealous of Big Buffalo that he is always warning us against him? He must know that we know the old rogue doesn't like us, and that is all there is of it!"

"Oh, I guess Fishing Bird means well; and I'm sorry enough that Big Buffalo isn't going with the war party. It may be that the chief's daughter has something to do with his remaining at home, but I do not think Fishing Bird is jealous. As for us, why the Buffalo has no reason to hate us on the girl's account. We never even spoke to her."

"But she has spoken to you, Ree."

"Never."

"Yes, she has—with her eyes."

"What nonsense!" Ree ejaculated. "Big Buffalo is ugly by disposition and has never forgotten the mistake I made when I overlooked him and supposed Fishing Bird to be in command of the hunting party I met that time they made me prisoner."

Presently the talk drifted to other subjects, especially to the disposition of the furs that had accumulated, and the plan to take them to Detroit now seemed the best to follow.

"But after all," Ree suggested, "we may be able to get a horse from the Delawares when Capt. Pipe and his men have gone."

"No, he is going to take all the horses. They will dance and feast to-night, and to-morrow they start," John answered.

"How do you know that?"

For a moment there was no answer; and then in a hesitating way, "Gentle Maiden told me," John confessed.

"Oh, ho! You've been making love behind my back, have you? When did you talk with her?"

"Why, there was no love about it!" exclaimed John with some pretense of indignation. "We were only talking as anybody has a right to talk. It was while they were dancing. And Ree, she speaks better English than her father. The missionaries among the Moravians who were massacred several years ago, taught her. And she thinks it was right that Col. Crawford was burned because of that massacre, too."

"I guess you have talked to the Indian girl before to-day, haven't you? Why didn't you tell me?"

"She spoke to me first, and I—I didn't think you would be interested."

Ree smiled but said no more. The canoe grated on the lake shore toward their home, and the boys took up their task of carrying it overland to the river.

"We will write some letters to send home from Pittsburg; for I still hope we will be able to take our furs there," said Ree, as they tramped along.

But in those days of more than one hundred years ago, as at the present time, none could tell what changes another sunrise would bring; and neither Ree nor John dreamed of the terrible danger which was closing in around them, the story of which is told in "Two Boy Pioneers".

THE END.
W.B.C.

20301425R00078

Made in the USA
Middletown, DE
22 May 2015